WILD WITH ALL REGRET

… deep as love,
Deep as first love, and wild with all regret
Tennyson

Natalie L.M. Petesch

Second Annual
Winner Swallow's Tale
fiction collection

Additional copies of this book may be had by sending $10.95 (paper) or $15.95 (hardbound), plus 50 cents postage to:

Swallow's Tale Press
P. O. Box 930040
Norcross, GA 30093

We thank the following magazines for permission to reprint some of these stories. Support literary magazines, for they support writers.

crazyhorse for "A Man Called Manuel"
New Mexico Humanities Review for "Heroes"
Kansas Quarterly for "Losses"
Snapdragon for "The Street"
The Greenfield Review for "My Future"
New Letters
The California Quarterly for "Love"
The New Orleans Review for "Zhenia and the Wicked One"
The Wittenburg Review of Literature and Art for "I, Constanza"
The Chariton Review for "Through a Glass Darkly"

ISBN 0-930501-06-3 library binding
ISBN 0-930501-07-1 paperback

Library of Congress Catalog Number: 86-60697

Printed in The United States of America. Typesetting and printing by CLS Printing of Tallahassee, Florida.

TABLE OF CONTENTS

Wild With All Regret

for Nick and Rachel

THE LIFE AND LETTERS
OF HANNAH GORDON

Sept. 2, 1929

L eah says you can still hear me and see me so if you can hear me and
see me I can writ to you, cant I? Why not. So this is for you.

I had thes bad dreams. They told me you had dyed. I did not now
what they ment so I jumped up and down on the steps of the funral
parler in my new shoes. I was suppsed to cry so I cryed. Then they shut
down the box and they carryed me away onlie becaus I was scaired, not
becaus I was missing you yet.

Every body was talking about the Marquette falling. I thought it
was the earth falling, on the grave, that they ment. But later I knew was
peple were loosing there money.

Oct. 31, 1930

My first Hallween. They dressed me up as a cat. I had big ears and a
blak tail and they painted wiskers on my face. I pertended I was
meow-ing. I went trick or tret, sometims I howled like a cat on Pa's fence
that he scaires away by shooting them. I got lots of kisses, butfingrs and
milky ways. One lady gave me a penny. One man gave me a nickel. He
sayd, I knew your mama.

Nov. 15, 1930

At first Leah cryed all the time after you dyed. Then she met
Marvin Epstein, you remember him, he is the one who still wears
nickers thogh he is 14 yrs. old. You told Leah nobody in America wear
thos things only English people and rich people. What I would like you
to explan is how you dyed. Did you now something bad was happning
to you? Did you grab Pa's hand or Cousin Roberta. It was in the
hosptial I now, but ther was a window, wasnt ther? Did you look out the
window? Did you see the angel standing ther, he bete his black wings?
Thats the way Leah says it was. She was standing in the hall they
wounldnt let childern not 13 yrs. old stay in the room but she could here
you she sayd. She sayd you were crying. I want to now if ther is time for

1

peple to cry befor the angel taks you.
 After that when we couldnt slepe Leah toght me a prayer,

> Now I lay me down to slep
> I prey the lord my soul to keep
> And if I dye befor I wake
> I prey the lord my soul to take.

I want to now did you wake *first*? Plese find some way to anser. I will be standing at the bedroom window (Front Street) every night at 7:00 p.m. exactly. I will consertrate on you.

Sept. 18, 1931

 Miss Doukas is teching us Reding and Writing. It is very fun and easr than any game. She gav me Three Gold Stars on my test. That is the best mark anybody can have. She asked me if my mothr or sister had already toght me to rede and write. I sayd no but when Leah use to play tic tac to with me she use to put ABCs in the box sometims and gav me her coloring books so maybe I should tell Miss Doukas but if I tell her maybe she wont put gold stars on my papers and if she didnt like me I couldnt go to Grade 1B anymor.

Xmas, 1931

 I don't like vacation time. Miss Doukas will not come back after Xmas. She is getting marryed. We cant have her for a techer then. She says it is because a marryed techer will have her own childern and cant take care of us kids in the homeroom besides. Miss Doukas says she teches reading, writing, spelling, aritmetic, and handwriting to her fifty children in Grade 1B. I will pass to 1A now.

Jan. 10, 1932

 I have a new frend. She is a colored girl named Ora Lee. Thats a funny name I said and she didn't like it. She said How come *you* to have a funny name like Hannah? If I was you I'd pick me a pretty name. She said she'd call me Tamar (she read it in a book). I agree it is pretty, but can I change it all by myself?
 Now we are frends thogh and I call her Lee and she calls me Tamar (she dropped the Ora part because she said it sounded like a mouthwash). I have practiced my new name for two weeks now and I like it. Ora says Hannah is old fashioned.

2

The thing I would like to know is why we have to ask You for everything. I know that You made the world but if You made it don't You know all about it, don't You know that Im going to ask You what Im going to ask You and why wouldn't it be just as esy for You to tell me rite away without my even asking You "Never mind asking Me to be happy, you can hav happiness, I give all my children happiness until a sertain age. Then I divide it up according to how good theyve been." I mean You know everything so plese tell me will I always be this misrble? If You mean *no*, make that cloud pass over the sun in the next five minutes. I will close my eys and wait.

The sun is out so maybe You are telling me that I will not be misrble all my life.

* * *

I have decided You can't promise things ahead of time becaus it's not fair. When I prey Please God make me beautful so peple will love me, and when I prey, Please let me get all l's on my Port-card so that peple will say Hannah is smart and not a dummy like her sister, You must feel You ought not to promise anything. Probly becaus we must all be asking You for the same thing.

* * *

They say I cry too esy and that I am selfish. They say I am clumsy (I spilled some stuff all over the table today), or I hav a Big Mouth or sit too long and They say that is bad for a girl it is not helthy. In Vitebsk* She (the woman Pa married now) never sat reding all day but scrubbed floors dishes pots pans clened poltry fish and geese and washed her cloths in a boiling tub. She showed me the tub that is the same kind as she use in Vitebsk and a scrub bord with sharp glass ridges. She showed me how to scrub my socks on the glass bord. She is going to show me how to fix the holes in them. With a thimble she says she carried all the way from Vitebsk, a small thing like a nut that holds the hole in place till you can fill it with thred.

*I looked up how to spell Vitebsk. It is in Poland.

Can't You plese ask her not to ask me to fix holes in socks. I hate to fix holes. I *do* like to plant the tiny onions and potatoes by the fense. But Im never asked which I like better to do. I try to stay out of the way because if they see me jumping rope or anything I have to here her say about the girls in Vitebsk that could sew and bake bread and clean a whole house. So Im always misrble and God that is why You ought to anser me so ther can be some hope. They say that reding has made me

3

sick in the head and I need to go to a Dr. to see if Im sick in the head. Also that sitting too long reding will mak it hard for me to hav babes.

But once She took me on her lap and rocked me and told me I was skin and bones and what would peple say if I got tb. They would say she is a Wicked Stepmother. I know she is not wicked. I have read about Wicked Stepmothers in all the fairy tales they have at the librerry and she is not like them. She is just an old woman and does not have any magic power but only clenes house all day for nine peple. I have forgot to say that she has four boys they sel newspapers. One is big and drivs a truk everyday. I help him write his books. He says I write neat and pretty like a girl. He has big hands and cant write neat.

No date

Dear Auntie Bertha, Thank you for the beautiful prsent. I like the yellow dress very much and wish they would let me ware it but they say I look naked through it and it is "too old" for me (the dress). I liked the nice card you sent too. I wish I could com and see you in Chicago. Why dont you com here sometime? P.S. I lov you because you are my mother's sister (in real blood).

* * *

Everybody is mad at me for writing Aunt Bertha that they didnt like the dress she sent because Aunt Bertha called Pa and said What kind of dirty people we got there to tell a young girl she looks naked.

Feb. 3, 1932

Pa says he has lost Everything and it is a terrible thing to have kids when you have lost Everything and so we have move to this place She bought once a long time ago when she still had a husband who hadn't gone away and left her with seven childern to feed and thats why she is old and gray because she use to have to tie the boys to the bathtub while she went downstars to work in the bakrey. I like this place it has a carpet on the floor and a bathroom with shiny walls.

June 2, 1932

I dont mine this new place in fact I like it because there are lots of kids to play with round here, they play hopscotch, jump rope, etc. Red Light is the most fun. You hid your head aganst the tree and dont peek. You call out 12345678910 Red Light, and everybody has to stop. Then

4

again, and hide. Then you go-seek them. You tag them, then run home. I am very good at this game because I hear better than anybody. I hear even the grasshoppers bumping into the big leaves on the empty lot where we play this game mostly at night.

I am lucky I hear so good because sometimes they put kids who cant hear with all the dumb kids, in Specials. Everybody would laugh at me the way they do Leah. Sometimes Leah says something and I think the same way but I look the other way if they laugh because I dont want people to think I am dumb too.

Martin says he is not happy in this place the school is bad he says. He wants to be a "scientist" and he says he cannot lern about the body chemstry here they dont have any "LAB". Sometimes I'm glad I am the only one young here in the famly. The others all work or try to find work. It is bad too sometimes but most times it is nice when Martin tretes me good and tells me I hav to be redy to work hard because there are no jobs now like there use to be even his friends are On Relief and are shamed to by groceries wher people know them. He says I should work in an office then I wont have to work so hard. He says he is going to work as a window clener at a Hotel in Cadillac Square. Also mama had started a small insurance policy for him so he will study at Wayne. The Unversty (sp?) is only about 30 mi. from here but he says Ha Ha they have no window clening jobs in Ann Arbor so how could he go to UM. His birthday is tomorrow. He will graduate from high school on his birthday.

* * *

Leah tried to have a party but Pa said we dont have enough for nine people in this house alredy so are we supposed to invite strangers off the stret to eat our food? Martin said they are not strangers they are my freind. Pa said a freind is somebody who helps you wash windows when you wash windows for seven dollars a week. So Martin told everybody to go to Belle Isle and meet them there but there was no picnic only we went swimming. I liked it very much.

Sept. 8, 1936

Something wonderful has happened! I am transferring to "Inter-mediate"! This means they are skipping me a grade and I will go to Northern High in about two years. In this new school they have all kinds of lights everywhere, the floors are shiny (not like at Sherrard). They have a General Science teacher who talks all about the woods in northern Michigan and knows all about everything. I have learned the classification of Animal and Vegetable Kingdoms. But my friend Lee was not double-promoted so she is still in Sherrard which makes me very sad, but I write letters to her. I wish she would answer me but it is like she thinks I have gotten snobby since I go to this new school. I am not snobby, she is the one who is snobby to think I would be snobby.

[?] 1936

Dear Lee, You should see our General Science teacher! He's so handsome and young and we are learning lots about animals and plants. It's really funny to think of yourself as an animal isnt it but I always knew there was a lot of monkey in us!!!

I want to tell you what happened yesterday. Yesterday I met this boy he is a year older than everybody because he had a "reumatic heart" and was home for one year and now he's at Intermediate, and you know what? He plays *golf*! I never met anybody who played golf before, have you? He has his own golf clubs he carries in a special bag and he asked me to explain the difference between the Direct Object and the Indirect Object which is easy for me because it is my favorite subject. So I did. Then he started to sing a song he learned from his father, "The Object of My Affection Can Change My Complexion From White to Rosy Red." I think I am in love with him because I am not doing so well in Miss MacClelland's class anymore. She says she is "disappointed in me that I am getting boy-crazy already and she thought I was one of the few girls in the class who was truly serious about her work." But I'm going to get a 100 on that vocabulary test tomorrow, you bet.

Nov. 11, 1936

Dear Lee, How can you say such a thing to your *Best Friend*? Just because I said he sang this song about his complexion doesn't mean I don't like colored people for my friend. You are my Best Friend and even though we have moved away from the Sherrard School District you will always be my Best Friend.

Tara (your name for me, remember?)

P.S. Did you see the Armistice Day Parade?

July 4, 1938

I was sitting on the stoop. The cars went by. They are so boring, always the same. But still Martin says he would like to have one. He's almost ready to give up Wayne U just so he can buy one. I wish I could go to Wayne, but Pa says he is getting old, how long can he work? I am young, he says, I have my whole life ahead of me. Besides, he says, I'll

6

get married, probably.

There are more jobs now than when Martin graduated. I have a job in an insurance office, typing envelopes. I get $12.00 per week. This is only until the regular girl comes back. My "employer" says that if Mary Mullen stays home with her baby, maybe I could stay here and work my way up. Because I can take dictation, they would pay me $15.00. I was thinking I would say Yes, because that's a good salary. And another thing is, they don't work half-day on Sats. the way most offices ask you to.

This a.m. I walked into the office. Mr. Moore handed me a directory with thousands of names: He said, A copy of our brochure is to be mailed to all the people in this book. I looked at it. It was thick as my fist. It was eight a.m. We are a "modern office," so we don't have only 30 mins. for lunch like some offices where it means you have to eat your lunch right there and you don't get out till 5:30 p.m. Here I can go downstairs to the drug store to buy something I want. Though I don't like to spend extra money for the drug store food. But it's good to get outside for a whole hour. As good as eating. Today I was not even hungry, maybe it was the names and addresses of so many people I don't even know who will never hear of me. I felt sick to my stomach, my head ached. The first winter snow started to fall. I was not yet ready for it, I walked out into the snow soaking my shoes. But the clean snow like tiny wafers after so many hours typing black and white addresses was like a feast. I walked up and down Woodward Ave. exercising. At the same time I was watching the clock in the window .... I thought, I am walking myself the way a person walks their dog, only no leash: *the leash is upstairs.* Even if I worked-my-way-up (I was thinking) where would "up" be? If I got to be a private secretary I could earn fifty dollars a week, I could be promoted to be a dictaphone operator, I would transcribe even confidential correspondence. I could have lunch in a nearby restaurant with the Top Level. I would not have to watch the clock in a window to see when my lunch hour was over: I'd only have to wait until the Top Level would look around for their hats or for their briefcases and then I'd know it was time to go back. Above all, I could walk myself an extra half hour or so at either end of the day.

I took the elevator back up to the office and finished off the day. The next a.m. I did not show up for work but went to Wayne and signed up for Modern History.

Instead of studying it, I'm *in* it: History.

December 15, 1941

It will be our first Christmas since it happened. The war I mean. The boys are in shock. They sit around asking each other, How old are you? Are you going to register for the Winter Term? Do you have brothers? I listen. I came to the U. to get away from the office, to learn something and meet people. Many here are nice to me, expecially the boys. But they are changing before my eyes. The boys sit with their chins in their hands, like Pa. The girls have a kind of *glitter* in their voices, I guess it's fear. There's fear everywhere, it comes out as Crazy Jokes, but what everybody is thinking about really is Who Will Die and Who Will Come Back?

And who will love us when all these boys are gone?

Jan. 31, 1942

Dear Mama, I said to him what is the use of falling in love if you're going to be going away? How do you know that? he asks. How do you know I'll have to go away. A lot of people stay right here in the States. Some even go to college, to UM. Look at all those guys going to be in the officer training program. Do you think you can be an officer, I said, because he was eighteen. He stared down at me. I pulled the blanket over me, because it was bitter cold in his room. As he dressed I could see how his body trembled from the cold. If the war lasts long enough, he says, everybody will be an officer. Even me .... He kissed me. I think we should get married, he said. I want to make an honest woman of you. Is that like being an officer I asked.

But I was happy. We argued about names, but I was firm. If it's a boy, I said, it'll be Alessandro Junior. And we laughed.

[No date]

I wonder sometimes, would you have wanted me to marry him. I think you would have liked him: he liked you, what I told him anyway. There's not much to tell about you is there, mama, like there's not much to tell about him. I don't talk to other people about him, just as I don't talk to them about you. Because they don't even know him. If I say Alessandro, Alessandro, it means nothing to them. They don't hear what I mean, the love. So I just say Yes, he's in basic training now. He'll be overseas soon, I guess. I try to say this with pride, but when I think how skinny he is, he's lost 20 lbs. already and that they've made him look like a porcupine with that hair and how changed he was when I saw him, I feel more like crying than anything.

October 25, 1942

Dear Alessandro, Your son was born at 12:05 a.m. He weighs eight lbs. 2 oz. and is twenty-one inches long. Guess he'll be tall like his father! I'm writing this from the hospital. The stiches hurt, but my heart is bursting with joy. If I live to be a thousand, I'll never forget how I felt to see him the first time. If only you can get leave this Christmas.

Dec. 1, 1942

Dear Alessandro, Well if you can't come here I'll meet you there. But the Dr. says little Alessie isn't big enough yet for such a long trip. He says it's risky in this weather. The trains are too drafty. Also that it's not a good idea to expose an infant to trains full of soldiers—"Soldiers carry germs" he says!!

So I will leave Michigan Central Tues. eve. and arrive in NYC next day at 11:00.

I dreamt last night that you were on a troop ship and everbody was listening to you like you were a teacher or something and you were saying (*isn't this silly?!*) "My wife has the most beautiful——" I don't know how to write about this to you because suddenly in the dream you were Home(!) and you were telling me this yourself and I was crying for joy. Then Alessie woke me up and as I stood by his crib I asked God, When is Alessandro going to see his son?

Dec. 29, 1942

Dear Alessandro, Yes, it was beautiful in the snow. The NYC shop windows decorated like churches. But the best time for me was when we stood outside the Cathedral and you sang to me, I'll never forget that song if I live to be a thousand. And you were crying. It's not that I wanted you to be crying, Alessandro, but I used sometimes to ask myself if you really loved me or just felt sorry for me and just then (at the Cathedral) I understood how much you missed me and Alessie and felt for the first time that we were *really* married, not just a soldier and a girl in wartime who you know got pregnant. Well, *you* know what I mean.

March [?]

Dear Alessandro, I'm sending this to your new APO. Your mother is so changed without your father. She never smiles, even when she sees Alessie. I tried to explain to her like you said that a soldier can't just abandon his duty, but she is bitter. She says, "Other servicemen have gotten leave to go to their own father's funeral my God." And just cries.

Nov. 1, 1943

Dear Alessandro, I can't believe it's almost Christmas again. If I had known the loneliness was going to last this long I couldn't have stood it. I know you are lonely too, in a different way. I have to tell you something in case some busybody does. I went out with Eddie Nyast's cousin, do you know who he is? Well, we went to a movie together, all four of us and then Eddie said why don't we stop for a beer someplace and so we did. I did most of the talking, that's what surprised me, I was so lonely I hadn't realized how long it'd been since I'd talked to anybody but Alessie. Then Eddie and his wife went home suddenly, I don't know why, I think they were quarreling, which left me and the cousin together (we left about a half hour later). I want you to know this just because there are so many busybodies in this world who spread stories and I didn't want you to hear it from somebody else maybe that they saw me sitting in the Pontiac bar with Eddie's cousin. I'm not sure how he spells his name, but you know the one. He works in the tool-and-die.

Nov. 12, 1943

Dear Alessandro, I'm sending you another pkg. Hope it arrives safely. The pictures of Alessie and me came out good, don't you think? The strawberry jelly fingerprint is his too! When he sees me writing he says, *Daddy, Daddy,* and jumps in his high chair like he knows where this letter's going. I haven't heard from you since Oct. I know the postman doesn't travel regularly from there to where you are but it does seem the U.S. gov't. could do better.

    P.S. Eddie's cousin got married. To that girl he met in New Orleans. "A whirlwind romance," she said.

[?] 1944

Dear Mama, It's been a long time since I've been able to write to you.

After they told me about Alessandro I guess I went a little crazy and didn't talk to anyone. The Dr. says if this kind of letter eases me, "Well why not?" He's a Well-why-not kind of Dr. if you know what I mean. I guess he's afraid to say yes or no and if he says Well-why-not, then whatever comes of it is nobody's responsibility. But I don't agree with him. I think that whatever comes of it is my responsibility. I sit and look at the snow falling. The snow falling in Detroit looks just like the snow falling in Russia, in France, in Belgium, in Italy, the same kind of snow covering tens of thousands of bodies. If the dead in this war were laid out end to end would they reach the moon? They say Alessandro was "mopping up" in Italy. What a strange idea. Like they'd sent him on a house-cleaning job. Just one sniper did it, not even like an ocean had swallowed him up. He always wanted to see Europe. If I live to be a thousand, I never want to see Europe. I hate Europe. Most of all I hate Italy. I will never let Alessie go to Italy.

Aug. 30, 1945

Dear Mama, They say I'm getting better. I don't feel better. I feel tired. They let me go "Home" for a week-end so I went with Leah to Alessandro's grave to lay some flowers there but they say I fainted. I didn't faint, it was just that I was tired. You probably want to know who's been taking care of Alessie, well to tell the truth I didn't think much about it at the time, maybe God was. Leah says you always believed God would take care of your children. Do you still believe that, I wonder. I wish you'd answer sometime, particularly here in this place. It gets awful lonesome here in this place where we walk back and forth, back and forth. Mostly they just listen to the radio or wait around for meals. For supper tonight we had a ham sandwich, a glass of milk, two olives and a piece of chocolate cake. As I swallowed it I thought, *A strange sweetness in the mouth, that's what being alive is.* Suddenly I could hear Alessandro singing in front of the Cathedral and I began sobbing and they gave me these pills that make you quiet. Ah what a rest they give you from the churning, churning.

Houston, Texas
Dec. [?] 1945

Dear Leah, No I'm not sorry I moved so far away from everybody. I needed a different world. And it is different here, that's one thing. Speaking of a different world, Lou Springer wants to marry me. He says he will be a good father to Alessie. He says a boy needs a father.

I feel I didn't thank you right before I left, for taking care of Alessie while I was sick. Although we disagree about a lot of things we do at

11

least agree about one thing, that it's important for the sake of the kids to keep your health. I hope Midge and Bernard are over the flu. I'm sending a picture of Alessie "helping" me.

Love,
Hannah

Christmas, 1946[?]

Dear Leah, Hope this letter finds you and your family well. Yes, I'm still working as a practical nurse, there's been a shortage of nurses you know Since The War (everybody uses that expression, have you noticed, like B.C. and A.D.) and so I keep busy. It keeps my mind off things. I like the work because I don't start until 4:30 p.m. That gives me all day with Alessie. You can't imagine how smart that kid is. I was pushing him in the playground swing, back and forth, back and forth, for an hour it seemed like, my arm was getting really tired. He kept asking to go higher and higher. Then he said, "That's enough. I saw them O.K." What he was watching were the seagulls flying. When he got home he did a picture of the seagulls (watercolor). I think he is real talented.

You asked about Lou Springer. I broke it off way last year because he said to me, "Well since she *offered*, it wouldn't be so bad for Alessie to grow up in a large family". "It's not so large," I said, not showing how mad I was, "my sister's only got two kids." But I thought that he was trying to separate me from Alessie, that he was jealous of him. So I broke it off. Or maybe I didn't really love him.

[No date]

Dear Leah, It's not so much the work, it's the long hours you know of being on your feet. You should see the veins in my legs they look like rope they're so swelled up, but I can't take a chance on operating because what if the operation didn't work or I was laid up for a while and couldn't work, who'd take care of Alessie? I just wear support stockings, they help some. It's not the feet anyway that hurts so much. What it is, is the loneliness. Maybe I made a mistake in not marrying Lou, I mean when I had the chance. I guess I was young and foolish and thought there'd be more chances. Well *yes*, there were a couple of others, but nobody really nice, if you know what I mean. And Alessie was getting too big to accept just anybody. He got tall so suddenly, it was already like having a man in the house, I just knew it wouldn't work. But sometimes when I'm coming in late I think how it would be to have somebody open the door and maybe help me ease up a little with some small talk you know about how the day went. But I do try to keep cheerful. After all I'm lucky I have my boy, lots of people don't have anything, I see them all the time, real sick and nobody comes to visit, nor writes them either, you'd think they never had any children.

I took out a pretty big life insurance policy, I mean big for me, it cuts into my pay considerable but a lot of strange things happen here at the hospital and it occurred to me what if something happened to me, who'd take care of Alessie? I mean I want him to go to college, not like Martin and me. You can't do anything without college anymore. And Alessie's got very good grades in Art and "Sociology" (they didn't even teach that in high school when we were kids, did they?) It's one of the best high schools here, in spite of some tough kids in the neighborhood. It's true he didn't get all A's, but I always felt there was something missing in that valedictorian (sp?) the one they nicknamed Sarah Bernhardt, you remember her? She married a Dr. But when Alessie walks on that stage to get his diploma, I can say, He worked for it, not like some I know, and I'll be proud as punch. I only wish Alessandro— well, there's no use talking about it. I got to go and wash my uniform and clean my shoes. There's nobody going to be on duty tonight but me and Mary Fein so it's going to be *busy*! One thing I'm glad, I'm not working at Children's. I tell you I just can't stand to see those kids, like the ones that have leukemia, they are so pathetic and God only knows how their parents live through it.

Labor Day, 1960

Dear Mama, I thought it was painful when *you* went away but I never thought Alessie would grow up and go so far away. I never thought a little thing like growing up would be such a big thing after all. I think I would never have left *you* if I'd been lucky enough to have kept you in the first place. So how can Alessie just go away when I never even let the sunlight fall on his face without my feeling it first, was it too warm? And it's not even a hardship for him, that's what I can't forgive, it's just to have fun and see Europe and see ... God help me I still can't even write the name of that place where Alessandro died, see *Italy*. They tell me Alessie will come home again that it's all a part of growing up, but I don't believe them. Why should a handsome young man with his whole life ahead of him want to stay home with a silly woman?

Sept. 20, 1965

Dear Leah, I'm a grandmother! I never thought I'd be so happy if I lived to be a thousand. It's like having Alessie back in my arms. Well, of course not exactly—Alexey takes more after his grandfather, and smart as a whip. As soon as I come in the door he tries to climb out of his high

13

chair calling Nanna, Nanna. If I don't pick him up right away he throws his spoon down to the floor and points to it and looks at me reproachfully but at the same time with a really *wicked* gleam in his eye as if to say, "*Now* look what you've made me do by ignoring me." So then I pick him up of course. What does amaze me is how big he is already. Did our kids weigh as much when they were Alexey's age? Or maybe it's me. Maybe my arms aren't so strong as they used to be. Still got all my own teeth though except one, and as long as I can stay healthy I thank God.

P.S. Next month is Alessandro's birthday. He would have been 42. That's hard to believe. I can only remember him as a young man, singing in the streets of New York, his hair the color of my wedding band. It makes me think sometimes: if there's a resurrection of the body, what will Alessandro have to say to this body, this *grandmother*? Well, I guess God will sort all this out for us, right? After all, Heaven's not a Social Club.

Hotel Dreyfus
Paris
Sept. [?] 1967

Dear Miriam, I didn't feel I'd said all I meant to on the phone, I'm following up with this letter. It was a terrible connection, you'd have thought we were on different planets.

Well, I ask myself, What can I tell you to give you courage? I love all of you so much. I guess I can't really understand those words, *honor, duty, moral obligation*, etc. I think I never taught Alessie to put his country above his own children. No, even if I'd believed it, and I did try to believe in it for Alessandro's sake—after all, we knew if Hitler won he'd have ruled for a thousand years—I still wouldn't have had the courage to *say* so to Alessie. Because Alessie was already to my way of thinking, *deprived*. Maybe that's it. Maybe it's because he's never known a father, maybe he feels he has to be as brave as he feels his father was. But maybe it *is* Patriotism and all and what he feels is his Duty and I can't deny that his father went to protect us all from Hitler, that he gave his life so we can enjoy freedom and maybe as you say Alessie feels he has an obligation to protect that freedom not just for himself alone. The truth is, *I don't know*. I've asked myself so many questions until I'm half crazy, but I don't have any answers. I pray every day for you all.

Will they deliver a package to him if I send him some things? Write and give me his exact address in Vietnam.

You have to try to *believe*. It's not a time to lose your Faith.

P.S. You know I never thought I could stand to see Europe. But it looks just like any other place to me now, not like the pictures I saw during World War II. Hard to believe there was an "Occupation" here and that people were arrested and never seen again .... I look at the faces of people my own age and wonder what they've been through. When they look miserable or mean I think to myself, *Don't* look like that! Alessandro died for you, so you and I could be *safe*.

But I won't go to Italy. I swore I'd never go and I won't.

Sept. [?] 1967

Dear Mama, What I wrote yesterday to Miriam is all lies. I'm full of a terrible rage. I want to blow up a building or something. I don't feel any pride in Alessie's going, none at all. To think that he didn't even have to go, he enlisted, that's what I can't forgive. It's like he threw our love in our faces, Miriam's love, mine, his kids' and said, *All of you, you're not enough. I have to prove to myself I'm just as good and just as brave as all those other men who're fighting for us.*

Maybe that's what they *say*, but I don't believe a word of it. I think they go because they want to go, that's all. And I hate him for it, that's the god's truth, Mama, I hate him for it. He didn't *have* to go and he went anyway so he doesn't give a damn about us, I mean how can he? It's like some minister who neglects his own family and the kids run wild and get into drugs and all the the time the Reverend Whatshisname is saying, I'm doing the Lord's work. And what work of the Lord is Alessie doing over there that the Lord wouldn't require of him to do right here at home, taking care of his own kids? So when Miriam said to me on the phone, *I hate him*, I understood exactly what she meant but still I said, "No, you don't really hate him, you're just saying that right now." Why do we always deny the truth? I think sometimes I hate you too, Mama, letting yourself die like that, as if there were *millions* of you. You should have *fought* it instead of going down silently for the third time like you were drunk on death and couldn't fight it. You had a responsibility to *us*, like Alessie. So I hate you too and I hate the government and I hate Alessie.

Next Day

I probably should not write such things, even to you. Maybe they don't do any good. Maybe it's better to go on pretending you have Sweet Thoughts because then you don't have so far to go back when you start loving again. Besides, if you say you hate someone they always believe you, they even believe you hated them all along, that your love has been a lie. But if you say you love someone they ask, How much do you love me? Or, How long have you loved me? Nobody asks *how much* and *how long* when you say you hate him.

Dear Mama, I was thinking so hard about this I had to stop to tell you. I just got a letter from Alessie and he told me he was well and safe and the year would be over before I knew it. And then I started thinking about how getting a letter from Alessie was like getting a letter from Alessandro used to be, only more so. I don't know if you ever felt the kind of love for our father that I felt for Alessandro, a love of the body I mean as well as of the spirit and then too you didn't live long enough to see Martin go away so I don't know if you can understand this. But let me try to tell you how it is: The letter is in the mailbox. You see the beautiful handwriting right away even before you get there. You take it out as if it were a living thing and hold it close to you. You rock it and kiss it as if it were still your child you had in your arms. Then you *open* it, and there are all those words that prove that he's alive, that it was not all a dream, that you really were young once and had a child that you loved more than your self. And the joy it, Mama, the joy of that letter is so pure. There's no body at all, it's a pure joy of love like spirits or angels joining in the air. It's like once when Alessandro and I talked long distance, there were only our voices, no bodies, just his voice, and his voice was his soul without the body. And maybe that's the way it'll be in Heaven when we all meet again, do you think?

Christmas, 1967

Dear Miriam, I've mailed two boxes of cookies, a woolen sweater, four pairs of socks with reinforced toes & heels, the pictures of Lori and Alexey we took at Thanksgiving and the two already-wrapped presents from Alessie's old coach Mr. Bernardson, who said he wanted to send Alessie *some*thing when he heard where he was. Also sent him some of that fungus medicine he said he wanted for his feet. The same kind he used at summer camp. Still, you'd think the army could supply things like that, I checked the label and it's just over the counter stuff.

fragment   April [?] 1968

Dear Mama I've got nothing to say to you. You already know it, Miriam already knows, Lori and Alexey already know it, the War dept. already knows, especially those murderers who sent the telegram, *they* know it. Maybe God's the only one who doesn't know, if there is a god which I doubt. If there *is* a God I want you to go to Him and tell him I spit in his face. A stupid Barbarian-God! A dog would take better care of

May 3, 1969

Dear Leah, Thanks for your card. There's nothing new to write. They say that people who grieve more than a year should see a psychiatrist. There's no psychiatrist in the world who can cure me. The people who wrote that are not grieving, they're writing about somebody else's grief.

I'm sorry you're having so many problems with your feet. Have you tried nurses's shoes? I've been wearing them for years now. When you have to stand on your feet for nine hours a day (or night) you need good shoes. It's getting harder to ride the buses though. I may get a car soon if I can save enough so that the payments wouldn't be too high.

Detroit
June 21, 1975

Dear Miriam, What would you say if I told you I'm thinking of marrying Leonard Weiss? It's not so romantic as you described (you were only kidding me I know) But it's so lonely here since Martin's moved to Arizona (he says it's been a godsend for his arthritis and all) and especially since Leah passed away last year. Maybe it was a mistake to move back north.

Tell Alexey all his fishing gear is still here and ready from last summer and also his wading boots (size 8 (!) all the men on his father's side do have big feet!!) Speaking of size I'll bet Lori is quite a young lady now and the bathing suit she forgot last Aug. probably will hardly fit.

Now that I have a car I can pick them up at the airport and we'll go straight out to the cottage.

Hope you and Hank have a good time on your vacation. You deserve it. I know it hasn't always been easy for you either.

Aug. 28, 1975

Dear Miriam, I don't know how it happened. I thought I was going to marry him. Then he was so mean with Alexey when we were in the boat, I thought I was going to just push him right out of the boat, to see how he'd like it! Now that didn't seem like the right attitude for a woman about to be a bride, so I just called the whole thing off. Also, I thought to myself I want this place to be *always open* to my grandkids, to be able to spend the whole entire summer with Alexey and Lori if I want. I'd lose my independence, what little I have I mean. So I backed off. I wonder if I did right. I wish there were some way a person could know ahead of time whether she did right ....

Dear Mama, I haven't written you in a long long time, partly because I stopped believing in god after they sent me back my boy and folded this flag in my hands, you know I still can't talk about it, but you know what happened. Anyway I even stopped believing that you could hear me after all, that Leah too was a liar and had told me these white Lies-for-children many years ago and I had gone on believing it like a child.

But anyway, suddenly I was going through a lot of old photographs and there you were still looking at me with those all-knowing eyes of yours and it was just like you'd *called* to me and said, How come you don't tell me things anymore? Maybe I'm just getting old and losing my mind. Everything seems to have some secret significance like the very skies are trying to speak and make meanings out of nothing.

July [?] 1983

Dear Mama, This is going to be my last letter to you I think. Because I am resigning from the human race. When Miriam called to tell me Alexey was in Beirut with the Marines I told her he was an idiot and she was an idiot too to ever have let him go in (as if anybody ever stopped them when they made up their minds). She said when he first signed up the Marines just seemed to him like an inspiring place to be. She said, It's not like it was with Alexey's father, he really didn't want to go, that he never expected to go where there was a war. She was crying .... Well, I didn't trust myself to answer, I was so angry. What was he thinking about, that they'd give him all that training and education and plenty of chances to impress the girls and then let him go off to vacation-in-Hawaii or somewhere? I was so fed up with the whole lot of them I didn't even want to talk about it, I tell you, Mama, I've changed. No patience anymore with the human race.

Aug. 7, 1983

Dear Lori, I'm sending you all these pictures we took at the cottage. You look so pretty in all of them. I thought maybe you'd like to send some of them to Beirut.

Love,
Grandma Hannah

Dear Mama, When she told me about the bombing at the airport I guess I fainted or something anyway one minute I was on the phone talking to Miriam and the next thing I knew a neighbor was taking me to the hospital. I'm O.K. now though I guess with this kind of thing you never know. Anyway I knew I had to be with Miriam, so I made them let me go, I knew where I *had* to be. It was the first time I was ever in an airplane and I didn't even remember to be scared. I just sat there the whole time praying, I'll do anything You want, I'll give up the rest of my life. Just let him be all right.

Then suddenly Miriam and Lori were at the airport to meet me and it was like coming out of a nightmare and we were all crying.

It was the waiting that was the worst. Every time we'd hear something new about it, the bombing, Miriam would look so scared and my heart would stop. I'd been through it, it was more than I could stand to be with her, but there you are, when you have to, you do. At last somebody from the gov't called and told us Alexey had "sustained some injuries" but that he'd be all right. We were scared that there was something else that maybe they weren't telling us. Miriam was so weak she could hardly pick up the suitcase she had ready to go meet Alexey wherever they said. I asked her did she want me to go along with her, she burst out crying and asked Could I stand it, that *she* couldn't stand it, she couldn't stand it. Then Lori said that when they told us we could go, we'd all go together, that's what.

[No date]

Dear Mama, When we arrived at the airport we couldn't stand being separated for a minute. It was like if we didn't all breathe together, Alexey would stop breathing too. So we waited, three half-crazy women. When it was nearly time for Alexey's plane to arrive I took my nitro. pill on the spot, I tell you it was not *convenient* for me to die just then, Mama, if you know what I mean, I knew I had to bear this with Miriam and Lori. So we stood there, the wind whipping our faces until *he came down the steps!!!* Mama, you should have heard the sobbing with joy that he had all his limbs, his beautiful legs, his arms, and his eyes .... We ran and kissed him, and had it not been a public place we would have knelt down and kissed all his beautiful living flesh. I can't tell you Mama how we felt. I only know it was the happiest moment of my life, he has some scars, they'll heal, and if I live to be a thousand I'll never forget the joy of that moment.

BENITO IN LOVE

Silencio. Then again Massif's hoofbeats, like the rain on the roof of their house: only fifteen kilometers from his village, and here the afternoon rains had already fallen. In the polished pools he could see as they passed: the vaulted sky, the cactus fence of a pulque farm, and the white crest of the volcano. From time to time Massif, had she turned to look, might have glimpsed herself in the gleaming surfaces: but she knew better than that. Sedately she made her way, her hoofs cleaving the water with such clean sharp steps that the mirrors seemed to break apart silently.

Benito wished he could have outfitted her more lavishly for the event. But he had paid a blacksmith a week's wages to have her shod, and he had not succumbed to the temptation of grooming her himself. He had bargained with his patrón for the use of his charro outfit, promising to work not only in his avocado fields but with the horses from now to Christmas. It had been a hard bargain: now, after buying new lariats, he had not a peso left. Though Boudreau had assured him that the lariats he offered to lend him were as strong as steel, Benito had preferred new ones: he knew better than his patrón that when the rope landed around the legs of the bull, nothing in heaven or earth should free him.

Massif's ears slanted cautiously: what she did not like were these automobiles hurtling toward Mexico City. Knowing this, Benito spoke as if he had heard her: "Well, let them go if they want, eh? Who needs them?" Massif listened attentively: she knew Benito's ways. Yet it was not he who owned Massif, but Boudreau, a former textile merchant from Lyons. It was Boudreau who had foreseen, as he sometimes boasted, that the little white palomino would be as strong as a mountain one day. At such times Benito too would join in singing Massif's praises: she was like a camel for water, she would stand with endless patience in the bullring while the sun became as sharp as hot knives on the skin. Then after an interminable wait, she would rouse herself to gallop at lightning speed, halting at the merest touch of the bridle on an imaginary line. During the *coleada* it sometimes seemed to him that Massif was as eager to taunt the bull as Benito himself. And with all this power, her legs were exquisite stalks.

Yet it had been neither her speed nor her temperament that had lured him to long labor for the pleasure of riding her, but her eyes .... Once, from among the rows of avocado trees where he had been working, Benito had glanced toward the corral. It was there, just outside the corral that she was standing when he first saw her: someone after riding her had neglected to return her to the stable. It was nearly sundown and Benito had been due home in an hour to celebrate his fifteenth *cumpleanos*. Massif was cropping the grass, eating not from hunger, it seemed, but with great fastidiousness, as if determined to show him what manner of horse she was: they had left her like this, sweating lightly from her exercise, but she did not complain. At the sound of his boots she had looked up. Her eyes were as soft as dusk, they filled him with their love and melancholy. In her eyes he had received for a split second the full shock of history: of Cortés rising on the horizon like a sungod or centaur, bringing to his people despair and salvation.

Now, as Massif passed a wooden plaque nailed to a tree, Benito rose slightly in his saddle. Someone had met his death at that spot, struck down by a truck: he glanced at the name and date freshly burned into the wood. Massif paused, one hoof in midair as if to avoid stepping on some living thing. Then she trotted on, assuring him by her steady pace that *all was well, all was well.* Her rhythm reminded him of the clock in Boudreau's dining room, ticking out life in tiny pieces: he muttered now to Massif that before God he did not envy Boudreau his great dining room nor all his wealth, but what he did envy him with all his heart was Massif.

To own Massif, from her cream-colored forelock above the damask eyes to her flawless white fetlocks, seemed to him something impossible or forbidden, like owning the sun or the moon. Yet the strange truth was, as Benito would complain bitterly to his mother, that although Boudreau could ride her from dawn to dusk if he wanted, he rode other horses instead: he claimed Massif had once turned skittish on him: "And you know, Benito, how careful you have to be when you ride a skittish mare ...." They had both laughed at the joke: the world was full of skittish mares and one rode them whether they were willing or not, one taught them what it meant to be controlled by powerful thighs and the bit in the mouth.

Though Benito had shared in the joke, he continued to believe that the problem was not Massif's. Boudreau had come to Tlaxcala to start an export business in woolens, but had turned instead to farming; he was not a real horseman, thought Benito, he liked to keep his feet on the ground, he was mainly concerned with his avocadoes which, when shipped to New Jersey or New York were worth their weight in gold. *"Equitacion,"* Boudreau had let him know, "with me is only a hobby .... In the old days maybe I could have been a *hacendado*, I would have sold my pulque in barrels, raised a few pigs, and bred a stable full of magnificent horses. That was the old days .... But the world is changing, Benito. When I first came here, I thought the big export was fabrics— wool, lace, all those things .... But there's more money in food. And much less risk too."

Benito had paused before placing a pair of avocadoes, green as

"God had brought them to this moment, he thought ...."

emeralds, into the filled basket. He straightened his back:

"Risk? Why risk?"

Boudreau laughed as if sharing another joke. "*Because*! People! People! More people every day, you can't count 'em anymore! People have to eat, they don't have to wear wool. Look at your Indians—do *they* wear woolen rebozos? Do *they* wear lace blouses? No .... They work to make serapes and lace blouses—for who?" Boudreau shook his head, patted his pockets for matches to light his cigar. "No, no, no. It's a big step backward for your country, I tell you. It's like Gandhi sending his people back to the spinning wheel. Was *that* what they needed? No," he answered himself. "Definitely no. What the underdeveloped countries need, Benito, is technology. What *Mexico* needs is synthetics." He tapped Benito's chest lightly. "*You* have the petroleum .... *They*," pointing vaguely North, "have nylon, orlon, acrylics, all the plastics ...."

Benito had listened to him with an air of deference. Though he had felt his anger rise at what seemed an insult to his people, he had controlled himself: Boudreau was a successful man, he had travelled much in the world, including the United States, and Benito was trying hard to learn something that would be useful to him. He would have preferred, even, that Boudreau continue lecturing him: but as so often happened, just when some harsh truth seemed about to fall into place—Benito's humiliated realization that day, for instance, that *Yes, it was true. We should exchange our centuries-old craft and our love of colorful design for combs and flashlights and transistor radios and tape cassettes and tv's and plastic shopping bags*—just at that moment Boudreau would wave him back to work.

... He surrendered himself now to the rhythm of Massif's hoof-beats; it was a sound which filled him with love, as soothing as the Latin Mass: "Dominus vobiscum ... et cum Spiritui Tuo ..." he began, but stopped at once. It must be a sin to recite holy words to a horse, even Massif. It was the second time that month that while riding her he had slipped into sin. Last Sunday a cassocked priest had darted in front of them, causing Massif to shy: enraged, Benito had shouted an insult. Later he had described the near-accident to his mother, vaguely hoping for maternal absolution. She had looked frightened, but controlling herself had managed a weak laugh to his Uncle: "That palomino is his sweetheart. He will marry her and I will have a grandson with four hooves ...." But his mother was wrong about Massif; Massif was not his sweetheart: he had a very definite girl in mind for his sweetheart. Her name was Juliana Gutierrez and she had been doing practice exercises for the festival when he first saw her.

He had been standing with Massif just outside the ring at Atlixco. The first time she passed him he had noticed how soft her mouth was and how the texture of her skin was not like velvet but like the soft beige of eggshell: her eyes reflected the sky. As she rode her sorrel sidesaddle

24

in the traditional manner of the charrería, she had seemed to him a perfect Spanish princess who would never be shaken. There had been a soft breeze that day and as she circled the ring, the hem of her skirt stirred slightly. Then on her third turn he had noticed that she was frowning; her sombrero had begun to slip backward, an awkwardness which, had it been an actual festival, would have cost her two points. The band of her sombrero had fretted a thin red line across her skin: in the tension of the moment she was biting her lip .... Benito shut his eyes, thinking what it would be like to have that mouth on his, bite for bite.

He had gone up to her afterwards, he had bowed ceremonially, imitating the elegant manners of a charro with a senorita. To these formalities Juliana had responded with a radiant smile. She had asked him his name. He had said Benito Valdez. She nodded in recognition, indicating a rancher in the crowd. "Ah yes, the Valdez of the pear trees."

He was shocked at her ignorance. The Valdez she had pointed out to him hired dozens of campesinos at harvest time. He, Benito, would have had to pick thousands of pears merely to pay for the spurs he wore—handcrafted serpents of silver coiled around star-like radii. But Benito merely bowed again, speaking of the beauty of her performance and her horse, Carita. As they spoke he saw how her face brightened; he drew closer to gaze with open admiration at the blue depths of her eyes. She began to speak more rapidly, with a certain breathlessness, about the beautiful day, Carita, her family, her friends in the nuns' school, till suddenly a tremor of shyness seized her and she stopped in mid-sentence, glancing around. Benito too glanced around to see what was troubling her, and realized with astonishment that the cause was none other than himself. He had understood at that moment that there was magic power in his own black hair and eyes: his heart had melted within him, for it was a power he had not known he possessed.

There was a long silence. With a nervous gesture Juliana had struck her palm lightly with her quirt.

"Ah, don't do that. You could hurt yourself," he protested with exaggerated concern.

She stared, struggling perhaps for words to put an arrogant Valdez in his place. Instead she smiled with radiant contrition: "You are right .... I never use it on my Carita, so why should I use it on myself?"

"Why indeed? A good mare needs only kind words. And many caresses," he added.

She had turned her head away, pointing to the sky. "It will rain."

Clouds were indeed gathering. In immediate collusion, without hurrying, they had turned their horses toward the Gutierrez ranch. They had much to say; it seemed they would never cease talking. They had been caught in the warm afternoon rains, Juliana laughing with childlike delight. At the gates of the Gutierrez ranch, although they were both wet to the skin, she did not ask him in. Benito understood that: he knew that he had already broken the rules by not introducing himself to her father.

They had arranged to meet again. It became an easy secret to keep since she rode out every day on Carita to practice for the festival, and so long as Benito made up the work, Boudreau was willing to let him go. Though Benito could thus spend many hours with Juliana he was torn between love and jealousy: Juliana could ride her sorrel in absolute freedom but whenever he rode Massif he was pawning away the days of his life like jewels. Then there were times when the work on the farm could not wait: at such times he would explain his absence to Juliana with excuses which surprised him by their inventiveness. He was sometimes troubled by this necessity, but felt it was not his fault: was he to give up Juliana because he did not own an orchard of pear trees? He loved Juliana, and she loved him. Indeed she loved him with a young girl's intensity which sometimes alarmed him: were it not for his own self-control they might both have fallen into sin. And for all her precocity with horses, Juliana sometimes revealed an ignorance so profound that he was both shocked and amused by it. He had once begun to explain to her how it was that Massif's bloodline was not absolutely pure; and although Juliana was the only girl in the *escuela primaria* who could tell a sorrel from a red roan at a hundred paces, she appeared not to know how or why it was that the mare was brought to the stallion. He had begun to explain it to her, but looking into her pale-blue eyes he had faltered: she had neither looked away nor blushed, but trustfully waited for him to continue. It had been he, Benito, who had quickly changed the subject.

Another time she had told him her father was coming to the bullring that day, that he and Benito would meet. Benito had objected, pointing out that it would be better to wait till Sunday after church or perhaps even after the festival. As Gutierrez's magnificent bay horse approached the ring from the highway, Benito slipped away unobtrusively to the outhouse on the hill. There he knelt on the floor watching through a crack in the wooden wall while Gutierrez chatted with Juliana. As he waited, a film of sweat had gathered on his back; a new depth of bitterness swelled in his heart: he knew he would never forget the slash of light illuminating the urine on the concrete floor, the skittering roaches .... At last Gutierrez had mounted his horse and gone.

In her innocence Juliana had accepted Benito's action as amusing. She had entered into the moment as a sort of conspiracy of the young against their elders: she had kept their secret. And today too, Benito reflected with irony, it would be a mixed blessing that he would have to return to the farm immediately after the festival, there would be no time for family affairs. He had already begun to weave an excuse for Juliana, explaining to her why he would not be able to join her after the festival, when Massif, knowing the way, accelerated her pace and brought them at a canter to Atlixco.

As they turned into the dirt road to the bullring, he saw that the festival was already under way. He rode Massif to a position on a hillside behind the seated audience. No one greeted him. It was puzzling till he remembered that he was wearing Boudreau's elegant outfit, including the sombrero embroidered with silver thread: perhaps he was not recognized. No matter: they would soon see who Benito Valdez was. He hoped for a bull of at least five hundred kilograms. That would qualify him for the maximum score: he vowed that he and Massif would gain every possible point today. He tightened the sombrero, he touched his lariats; a fragrance of rope rose in the air like incense.

The view from the hillside was excellent. A new performance had begun: he could see it all perfectly. The audience was seated on stone benches as in an amphitheater. Some were buying soft drinks, others were carrying pillows to ease the shock of stone on their spines. They were a quiet people, they had known each other for years, perhaps generations. They knew that loud shouts of favoritism were in low taste. When they called out their admiration, it was for some anticipated excellence—the premier performance by an eight-year old girl, or the performance by a great charro like Fonseca from Ilita. Fonseca's *cala de caballo* added up to a perfect score, the crowd applauded with joy, but there was nothing wild in their applause: above all, they were ladies and gentlemen. It was as if Benito had never taken in this astonishing detail before: he who passionately loved their horses had scarcely observed the people who rode them. He perceived now, with an intense and sensuous pleasure, their fashionable suede jackets, their embroidered dresses; he noted how the chestnut-colored hair of the women both young and old gleamed in the sunlight, and how the proud bearing of their men seemed wrought in their very flesh. When they walked it was as if they still stood high in the saddle: they held their backs straight, the breathing of their chests awaited the adornment of military medals. Above all, they spoke an educated Spanish which resonated in the air like oboes, registering a power and a pride that needed never to raise its voice .... And Benito too felt a momentary thrill of pride at his own earned presence there ....

But now, even as he noted the horses coming into the ring for the next event, something mysterious was happening to his vision. Suddenly the crystal frame of air, the blues and greens of the mountainside merging with the ceramic sky, all seemed but a marvelous painting such as he had seen once in Veracruz: and it was as if he, Benito, were also in the painting, that he could exist only so long as he was walking past the landscape, seeing himself in it, no longer. When he had turned a corner of the museum, glancing over his shoulder at the gorgeous gilt painting of *hacendados* mustachioed in the style of the great revolutionaries, their gold and silver regalia glinting in the sun like foxfire—at that very moment all this, himself included, would disappear ....

Still, he could not say that he was made melancholy by the vision. He was excited, rather; he looked forward to the competition as though it had been his wedding day. The events were going more quickly than he could have anticipated. The schoolgirls' *Escaramuza Charra* with which Juliana and her girlfriends would ordinarily have concluded the festival had been pushed ahead for some reason. He drew closer to see if something had happened to make this change necessary. But no, there was nothing untoward; they had not even bothered to announce the change, trusting that their audience would accept their judgment in such matters.

Massif, like himself, quickened with attention. Within moments Juliana and her friends had filed out into the ring. There was a reverent hush at the spectacle of so much power and beauty. Benito, too, though he was accustomed to it, was struck with admiration by the extraordinary performance of the girls. They seemed delicate as butterflies, yet they rode like Amazons. Most were very young, not yet in their teens. He hoped that Juliana's extra years of experience and even, perhaps, her more mature physical strength would give her an advantage over them.

Again, as always, he admired Juliana's breathtaking horsemanship: he never wearied of watching her graceful body as she flowed by, always in perfect control of Carita. Today, also, she began her performance with impeccable precision; she sliced her horse through diagonal lines, cutting and crossing and galloping at such speeds that he too stood breathless: a few millimeters difference could mean disaster. The crowd sighed with admiration. It seemed that today Juliana would transcend herself. But no: he saw now that though she was superb, she was also tense. Her many hours of practice had brought her through her first maneuvers without a fault, but then distracted for a split-second by some inner music, she allowed Carita to raise her head too high and thereby lost a point. Still, thought Benito, she will do splendidly yet, she will triumph. He found himself watching with a strangely detached curiosity as horses and riders began lining up again. The crowd leaned forward. Benito saw Juliana open and shut her eyes three or four times rapidly, as though trying hard to blink away a particle of dust. While backing up Carita, readying her to gallop, the line of her horse's movement seemed to Benito straight enough—but perhaps for the judges who measured with a more exacting eye, it would not have been straight enough. If not, then she would have lost another two points. But he was not sure now.... Though another infraction would be bad, it would not be hopeless. She could still complete the event with honorable mention. She had resources she could draw on—four years of riding almost every day, her near-mystical foreknowledge of Carita's every movement. They had readied their horses, they were dashing with incredible speed, all the horses seemed flying in opposite directions, like intersecting windmills.

Benito was mounting Massif for his own performance when he heard a murmur from the crowd, short deprecating cries of sympathy followed by a light burst of laughter, immediately hushed. Juliana had lost a spur: four points for the infraction. Her performance would be rated Poor. The girls in the *Escaramuza* were already galloping to the exit gate as Benito rode Massif into the ring for his event.

As they entered the ring, Massif moved sedately, though she, too, must be thrilling, he felt, with a shared excitement: she too had seen the great bull. It occurred to Benito that it was a stroke of luck to be following the girls whose horsemanship was dazzling, but also ornamental. The spectators would be more ready for a performance of pure power and daring.

He approached the bull with an almost casual ardor, a sense of their common fate: God had brought them to this moment, he thought, and he would bring the great *toro* to his knees; he would pull his tail in absolute defiance: he would pull Death's tail. Directing Massif with perfect control, he felt a thrill of power such as he had never known. He embraced Massif's flanks with his thighs as though he would crush her, he bore down with his full strength in the stirrups, he raced toward the bull. He leaned down from the saddle; through his right hand he could feel a surge of power, of ruthlessness, such as the hungering wolf must feel as it seized an antelope from the running herd. With his bare hand he gripped the *toro's* tail; though the bull had the strength of ten he, Benito, would bring him down, he would force his will upon him: within seconds the *toro* had turned and lay on its side. Then with a renewed burst of speed Benito galloped away, giving the bull just time to rise and run again before Benito, with perfect precision, looped his lariat just below the knees. Seconds later the bull was being dragged from the ring: Benito had conquered his adversary, not once but twice ....

He felt a fierce elation: he had ridden with the best of them and he had won. Several women, one of whom resembled Juliana, rose to their feet, calling out in admiration. Benito bowed graciously to them, but already the taste of victory was turning bitter in his mouth as he reminded himself he must hurry back at once to Boudreau's farm .... Before leaving the festival he covered Massif with a blanket: she gazed at him with ineffable love, sharing his triumph. Then they rode back to the avocado fields.

He found Boudreau in high spirits when he returned. "Ah, you made the festival come alive today, Benito," he congratulated him. Then as if to make it clear that the festival was over, he began showing Benito, in a voice serene with authority, the many jobs that remained yet to be done. Even while his patrón was talking, Benito began counting up the numbers: he owed Boudreau so many hours of work that when he looked at the calendar in the stable, the black figures seemed to blur and march and collide like prisoners in a crowded yard. He would be in debt until long after his Saint's Day. He would have nothing to spend at Christmas. And every joyful hour spent with Massif would sink him deeper into debt. He felt suddenly that instead of having won a victory today, he was a gambler who had lost a fortune.

He was brooding gloomily over these bitter truths as he worked in the stable when he looked out at the corral and saw Juliana with Carita. For some reason her presence there only deepened his bitterness: the thought that so much love was being offered him when he had not a peso to keep body and soul together, made him want to cry out in rage. It also occurred to him with alarm that Juliana may have heard him being ordered about by Boudreau. His anxiety made his voice diffident as he greeted her.

She too appeared anxious. Her voice trembled. "It is late," she murmured. "They do not know I am here. They will be looking for me .... I only came to say .... I wanted to say .... You were magnificent today, Benito, really magnificent." Her eyes filled with tears. Then suddenly, with a shy glance around her, she said she would like to see the horses. She touched his shoulders as he stood beside her horse. Benito took her hands in his, she was trembling. It became blindingly clear to him at that moment that she was longing, longing like any *perdida* in a cantina, to be kissed, to be kissed into a delirium ....

But suppose Boudreau should see them? He was filled with such anxiety at this thought that he did not at first move to embrace Juliana, but stood as if humbled and overcome by love. It was Juliana herself who slid from the saddle into his arms. As she kissed him, his eye was caught by a small dark stain on the saddle, a stain no larger than a copper centavo: his head reeled with the revelation. It was as if suddenly he were on a hillside and some pale messenger had come to reveal to him the true power and significance of his love. Inspired by this revelation and his own daring, he kissed first her hands, then her arms, then her throat and breasts, feeling a great surge of pride at the heat of her small body responding to his. His biting mouth on hers sealed a solemn prophecy: that this drop of blood would bring a proud Spanish family to their knees, they would beg him to become one of their breed, they would offer him orchards and spotless white sheets which he, Benito, for the sake of the family honor would conceal from the eyes of the curious; that this coppery stain would be a lariat more binding than steel, it would hold her fast in sacramental bonds even as he now bound her body to his with his kiss of love.

THE STREET

The tourists think I'm some kind of idiot, but I'm not. I understand everything they say, about me and about other things in the Quarter. Sometimes on a sunny afternoon on Bourbon Street their laughter will carry from across the street where they are standing in front of Marty's sign: Five Beautiful Girls—A Show Every Hour. (They're not all beautiful. Only La Sylphe.)

I can always tell when the tourists are no longer looking at the girls' pictures but are looking across the street where I am; their laughter stops, there is a sudden silence. That is when I know they are looking at me.

Usually I take my place in the street across from Marty's Place about dark. Sundays across from St. Louis' Church is not a bad place either, but in Jackson Square you have to compete with the artists; on Bourbon Street I only have to compete with Duke. He taps. Sometimes he picks up so much coin he can't go on tapping, else it falls out of his pockets. The tourists like to throw small coins like confetti, and they like to see the Duke pick it up. It's like they've been down on their knees all their lives making it, and now they can say: "Here, see what it's like." When the Duke gets too much coin in his pockets, he pretends he wants a beer and goes in the Red Barn where the bartender knows him. The Duke gives him a tip and, there in the back where nobody can see him, they turn the coin into folding money. That is one way. Every street beggar has his way of turning coin into bills. My way is different.

Everybody likes laughing at the Duke; he acts old-timey, like Hip Williams in Les Caves. He sings real nigger-style, a kind of hopped-up Fats Waller. He makes a mint, that Hip. And Duke and Hip, sometimes they do a team. They go right up Bourbon, down Royal and back through Chartres, tapping, singing and tambourining, like slavery was the latest invention of the tourists. Daytimes, they go to Tulane.

I started to go to Tulane myself once because I wanted to get off the Street. That was before I started saving my money. But I've only got one hand that's good and it's rough getting up the steps, especially without a ramp. You've got to have somebody to push you everywhere. One time the kid who was supposed to push me didn't show up, and I sat there in the snow a whole hour. I was covered with it, there was no one in the street to get me up the steps. I had pneumonia two weeks that time, and after that I came back to the Street. If you make enough money you can get off. That is the only way.

My place on Bourbon Street is a good one. I give Hawaii Jim half my take and he lets me stay in front of his place. If I get a bill I can tuck it away in my underclothes, but coins are harder; they jingle, and when around four a.m. they pick me up from the sidewalk and put me in my chair, the money will fall out sometimes. Hawaii gets mad at me then. He'll throw the money at me and yell "For cryin out loud, if you're gonna be a thief, why don't you get in the big time?" It seems on those mornings when they catch me with extra dimes or quarters they always have trouble getting me into my chair.

My problem with the chair is a special one, and they know it. When I'm down on the sidewalk, it's O.K. The fact that both legs are twisted in opposite directions gives me a kind of balance. I mean, that way I am pretty solid on the ground with the weight on my thighs—Duncan Phyfe they call me. My left arm is good for resting on too; it doesn't bend, but holds me up straight as a post on the sidewalk. By some odd coincidence, when it formed, the palm curled cuplike. This gives me a big advantage with the tourists.

Why they think I'm an idiot is because of the "major bone deformation." It kept the jawbone from growing and, later, when the teeth came in, there was no room for them; so the mouth won't shut and that makes the jaw look slack. They gave my mother free powdered milk and cornmeal and lard. There was no Vitamin D, they told her later, in the milk. She worked in a laundry nights, and slept days and we didn't get any sunlight, so it is only rickets, not polio. That was thirty years ago. Now they put things in, even in those CARE packages, so nobody has rickets anymore.

Truth is stranger than fiction. I heard once that a mother let her baby starve even while it was sucking the blood from her breasts. She didn't know the baby wasn't gaining weight. That was a long time ago in my grandmother's time, and nobody is that ignorant anymore. But the baby died anyway.

I have powerful hearing though, and I wear strong glasses so I don't miss a thing on the Street. The right eye slips, what they call walleye, and that makes me look funny. Years ago when I got my full growth, an operation might have straightened it out. The optic nerve it is. But at that time I'd really just begun saving my money. Because I wanted to get off the Street. I thought, if you save enough money, you will be free. If you have money, you can buy anything. People will shake your hand even if it feels like driftwood. So until La Sylphe showed up at Marty's Place about two months ago, it was like I'd been thinking of just one thing all my life: how to get off the Street. Then when La Sylphe started doing her act, I found that the Street could give you a bitter kind of pleasure. I mean if you cannot have the one thing you want, some other thing—like a woman—can make you stop wanting it, at least for a while. That is why I began thinking of money not only as a way to get off the Street, but as a way, just once, to get La Sylphe. I tried to increase my take. I even began to wear dark glasses and clothes that did not

match, like I could not see what to put on. That picked up business a lot. It is funny but if a tourist thinks you cannot see, he thinks you cannot hear either. I have heard strange things from tourists on the Street.

But if you want to know how I really feel about tourists, I'll tell you. I hate them. They've got feet and still they walk all over you. They stumble over me where I sit on the sidewalk, and I can't get out of their way. They walk around drinking "pinkies" from those Pat O'Brien hurricane glasses, and the first thing I know they're in my lap, glasses and all. When they break one of those glasses, I have to sit in the splinters all night, the sidewalks are always too crowded to hose down at night. It's the tourists who dirty up the street so we have to have a law in the Quarter for the residents to clean their sidewalks every day ... gum wrappers, straws, cigars, napkins, Kodak film, rotting flowers—whatever falls from them they drop in my street. But in the morning, when they go back to their hotels, the beautiful colors of the Vieux Carré come out again, like after a rainy night, the rainbow.

Then the children come out to go to school. They come by in maroon-colored uniforms and knee socks and file by me to the nuns' school. Some are scared of me and cross over to the other side of the street when they see me. But Amélie Godchaux is my friend. She taught me to play piano with one hand. That is the thing in life I like best to do. One day I pushed my wheel into the Old Slave Patio; they had a piano there, waiting to be moved. Amy taught me F A C E. Then she taught me to play something by Joseph Haydn. It was simple and I liked it, and Amy cried. I asked her why she cried, and she said it was because I played the notes so beautifully. In my room, though, there isn't enough space for a piano. So what I wanted was to get an accordion. An accordion is different. You can peg one side without needing to bend your fingers much, and my right hand really is strong. If you lifted me to a bar at the gym I could hang my whole weight on it. I can rest my weight on my arm and not even tremble. So I could probably learn to play an accordion real good. There are places where people sing and play the accordion. They don't pass the hat either, but get paid a regular salary, like bank clerks.

Amy would have liked that. I know she did not like me to sit in the street, especially when it rained. Sometimes she would save out something for me from her lunch box and give it to me on her way from school. I did not want it—I am never hungry—but I took it to please Amy. She would smile. She had small white teeth, like they were baby teeth, but they weren't; she was older than that, though still a child.

That was the trouble. Amy was good, but she was only a child. No body yet. I mean she did not suffer from it yet. She could never have guessed what I suffered because of La Sylphe. While Amy was asleep, dreaming of dancing lessons, I would be watching La Sylphe from where I squatted on the sidewalk, knowing I would die if I never had a girl like La Sylphe.

Between the two girls, there was probably not ten years difference —years like a lifetime. Listening to Amy in her white knee socks and parochial school uniform as she chattered about ma mère, mon père et ma petite soeur Lisette, was like being in Church. Watching La Sylphe was like being in hell. Yet both gave me pleasure—I did not want to give up either.

La Sylphe was the best stripper Marty ever had. She came from Nebraska, she never said what town. She told me later this was her first job, and that the other girls hated her because she was young. When the harvest was in, she told me, she and her father used to sit around and watch TV shows till early morning. One night her father seduced her. When the men on the next farm found it out, they used it against her, to make her give in, or else they'd tell the school principal, they said. Of course they told anyway. The mother had run away long ago with another man.

That is the way they all start on the Street. First cornfields and love, then the slow rot. But La Sylphe was a long way from rotting when I met her. She told me she had been working at Marty's only a month, when she first talked to me. That was about Easter time.

I could always see her plain as day from where I sat in the Street because Marty kept his doors open, just like they all do in the Quarter, so the tourists will gape at the girls. Then Marty would shame them. He'd say: "A new show every hour. No minimum, no cover. But don't stand in the doorway like that. Only bums do that." So then they would come in and pay two bucks for a six-ounce beer. And you had to drink up, you couldn't just sip it.

Marty always saved La Sylphe for last. First that brunette one would come out; she would have on a black nightgown, and gradually she would take it all off, except those T-shaped panties they wear and a pair of gilded horns on her breasts—no straps or anything. When the tourists are not standing right over me, I can see them all: Five Beautiful Girls. There's Allumette and Bonnie Belle (she doesn't work steady, though) and there's Slipper Ann, sometimes called Slippery, who has a thing about shoes and owns more than a hundred pair. Then comes the girl who does the Hawaiian pineapple strip, Aloha, and Tortoise-Shell, called that, the guys in the Quarter say, because she has such a hard back.

Then came La Sylphe. When she came out on the stand the men would croak like frogs. I've seen them come back night after night for a week—dead-looking men with gouged-out eyes, pushing their fat stomachs up close to the bar, and glueing their eyes to her like they were stone drunk, only they weren't. Sometimes they would bring their wives with them, scrawny women from their own hometown who didn't know the score, who never understood that the men were not thinking of them afterwards in bed at all—but of La Sylphe.

I thought of La Sylphe too. I thought of her every night. I would fall asleep thinking of her breast under my hand. Or of her belly; it had a white streak all around it, like lightning had struck her once, and the curve of her back was like horseflesh. I would just lie in bed and sweat, thinking about it. Then one night I dreamed she came to my room and said, "You're not a bad guy for a cripple." That was when I decided to use my money to see if I could get La Sylphe. For years I'd been saving it, nickel by nickel, quarter by quarter. Then dollar by dollar. That is why I never moved from my room on Dauphine Street. It was the cheapest room in the Quarter and every now and then the Vieux Carré Commission of New Orleans would talk about tearing the building down and "restoring" it, patio and all, but they never did, so I stayed.

In the first place, I had a gas burner there on Dauphine Street, and the bed was low enough for me to get in by myself. All I needed to do was grab hold of the metal bar and haul myself in. It was an old metal bed, and somebody had sawed off the top part of the legs to make it more modern. That is where I kept my money.

I bought some elbow plumbing pipe, to slip into the hollow legs of the bed, like one empty can will fit into another. Pieces just one inch in diameter fit perfectly. I told the guy I was going to make a new kind of rat trap, and he just laughed. "Sure need 'em around here," he said. The pieces fit very tight inside the legs of the bed, and it would have taken a strong arm like mine to wrench them out.

Nobody would of dreamed that a beggar like me would have had all that money. But I was careful. I never drank or smoked, and winters I slept in my clothes to save on heat. And always I thought, if you save enough you can get off the Street.

Al would come by in the morning to put me in my chair. Al is a World War Two vet. He was cut up a lot and he's not much good for anything, but he would come help me into my chair mornings. And sometimes we would have French coffee the way he liked it, strong. I made it myself. I did all my own cooking. That saved a lot. I ate canned soups a lot; you can add things to them, like beans soaked overnight, or hominy grits. And there's plenty of cheap fish in New Orleans—catfish, herring, squid. I got so I could bone a herring so it would fit right in the skillet, flat as a pancake. So I got along all right before La Sylphe came up to me that time. And I didn't just live on fish either. I had a metal box-stove, the kind you slip right over the burner, and one time Al and I baked a lobster he swiped at the market. We laughed a lot that time and weren't lonely. Because that is the main thing, feeling lonely.

That is why when La Sylphe crossed over to my side that morning about dawn, it was like the sun fell into my lap. I looked up at her and for a minute I was so scared I couldn't say anything. My first thought was that she knew all about how I'd been watching her and thinking about her and that she didn't like it—that she was going to tell me to change my spot on the Street, I was getting on her nerves, something like that.

But she just stood up straight and tall, like a runner taking deep breaths. She had on those tight pants they wear when they're off-stage, and high-heeled wedgies without straps to them, and a red sweater that was no sweater at all. She said: "Did you see a big, heavy guy out here—he had a camera with him, took moving pictures?" She checked her watch then, a big watch with leather straps like a man's. The man she was looking for was obviously a tourist. No guy from the Quarter would lug around a camera, especially in a night club. But anyway I hadn't seen any such person, and I was always aware of the finks who hung around waiting for her after work. More often it was just her guy Batchelli who picked her up. So my guess was, the guy hadn't waited for her at all, but after taking some pictures of her had lost himself in the crowd. I could see she was disappointed and I thought right away, maybe this is my chance. She might never get up that close again.

I lowered my voice so nobody else in the Street would know that she was getting fixed up with a street beggar. I was afraid if she thought anybody'd heard us she'd have to say no out of pride.

When I made my bid I saw her gold-colored eyes flare up like the painted blue edge around them had caught fire. I could see she could hardly believe a guy like me would have so much. It made me feel real good, like I was doing something big.

"Where do you live?" she asked with a funny look, scared and hurried, as if taking that much money was some kind of crime and she was afraid she'd be caught.

I gave her my number and the time was set for four o'clock, a good two hours before we went to work on the Street. I wanted plenty of time, because I knew she would need to get used to me. The last time a woman saw me undressed was at the county hospital, when I had pneumonia. The nurses kept changing every day, like they couldn't stand the sight of me. Then there came one who'd been working in the terminal wards. The first day she made a point of undressing me entirely and she stood there staring at me a while. Then she rubbed the S-shaped bone in my chest with her little finger and said, as if nobody was there to hear her: "It's just like somebody took him and twisted him right around ...."

Once La Sylphe had agreed to come, I tried to keep her standing there a minute talking to me, so that maybe Hawaii Jim would see us just talking together, like friends. But she was already looking up the Street, clutching her big handbag in both hands, like she was afraid someone would grab it. I noticed then that her hair was not really gold-colored like her eyes but that there were dark roots, like shoots pushing from the earth. A small line of impatience or maybe it was anger at that guy with the camera, had formed above her mouth, one of those deep lines that later gets to be like creased leather in greedy old men. But she was beautiful to me ... especially her hands, which were long and straight and the pointed nails were painted white, like moonstones.

"I guess the dirty liar's gone," she said at last.

Her still thinking about that tourist made me sick-jealous, but I just laughed as if I really did think I was God's-gift-to-women, and said: "That's all right, honey, you got me." I thought she might laugh or put her hand on my head or come back with a real snappy line, like a trooper. But instead, she looked down at me like she could spit, then she started clicking away on her high heels as fast as she could go. I watched her legs from where I sat, strong curved instruments, made of ivory.

"See you later!" I called after her, casual-like, but it was meant to close our deal.

By the way she looked at me I knew I would have to show that money the moment she got there. So I went home and pried loose the pipe from inside the bedpost, which I hadn't done in years. I even took out some rolls that hadn't been touched since I first started on the Street. I noticed then that the bed was beginning to rust a little and some of the bills had a powdery feel. The weevils had eaten through the newspaper I had stuffed in at the top, and had even penetrated some of the older money, some that I got when I first went on the Street.

I took it all out, all the bills, and cleaned them carefully with alcohol. I rolled the fifties tight toward the heart of the roll—I keep them tight as spools of tape, the twenties and tens on the outside. That way, even if there was a fire that melted the bed, the big ones would be saved. You know a book will burn on the outside, then snuff out toward the middle. In the other leg of the bed I always kept my cash till I could change it to bills at the bank. I went only once a month, to a different teller each time, so they never caught on how much money I had. Maybe I could have left the Street years ago but I wanted to be sure that when I left I'd never have to come back.

But now I needed a lot. After all, I figured La Sylphe had expensive tastes. She was used to being taken to the La Louisiane and Antoine's and Galatoire's and all those places I'd never been. She'd probably want a drink first, I thought, the best Scotch or maybe brandy. Maybe I'd better have both .... And then I'd have dinner brought in, like they do in hotels. But the main thing was to have the place clean, so I asked Al to help me. He pretended not to notice anything as we put on new sheets as white as milk and I made him empty all the trash around, even in the halls. Then Al gave me a good wash, all the time pretending not to see what was going on. I didn't want him to be there when she came in, though, so when it got to be nearly four I hurried him out.

I was so nervous I kept breaking out in a sweat till I worried about the wash Al had given me not doing me any good; so I tried to calm down by counting the squares in the linoleum; but one shape just blurred into another and I couldn't make out what I was counting. I noticed at the last minute that my nails were not clean and I was in a panic to get them clean by myself. But I finally did.

About this time there was a gay little tap-tap on the door. It was

Amy, of course. She always taps that way, like it's a game we're playing that maybe I got up and walked away. She said there was a real old-fashioned organ-grinder with a monkey parked in front of the French Coffee House: would I like to see it? She said maybe an organ-grinder really enjoyed playing his music, the monkey was so cute, he must be company for the Italian guy with the handle-bar mustaches. She asked me did I think he was really Italian? I could see what she was driving at, but I just said angrily that when I left the Street I was going to leave it for good, I wasn't going to go tinkle-tinkle around the country with a trick monkey and a fake handle-bar mustache. I said I was tired of fakes, even myself. I said I was a fake too.

She took my good hand and looked at it. "You have such a strong hand, Billy," she said. "I bet you could hold me up flat and lift me to the ceiling."

There was something about her calling me Billy at that moment that made me almost sick. It was as if I'd forgot my name was Billy and thought it really was Duncan Phyfe. And besides I was mad at her for taking such a damnfool time to come in, so I said, "Yeah, a strong hand like that could be very useful. I could get a job holding the torch for the Statue of Liberty."

She looked me full in the face then, very strange, and then those straight-out eyelashes, like a doll's, shut down over her face like the Quarter itself, sliding down all its beautiful pastel shutters, closing to tourists. Then she picked up my hand and cradled it a minute like a baby. "Billy-Billy," she said.

Then I could hear La Sylphe's wedgies clicking out in the yard. "Run along now, kid," I said, my throat like clay. "I got things to do." So she went. I don't know whether she saw La Sylphe coming up the old patio or, if she did see, whether she had any idea where La Sylphe was going. Anyway, the sight of La Sylphe put Amy completely out of my mind.

She wasn't dressed up or anything. In fact, she was wearing a kerchief over her hair, and slacks and carrying a small purse in her hand, like she was trying to let on she'd just slipped out to the grocery. Before she could say anything I handed her the money, and I saw the deep line above her mouth soften into a shadow as she counted it. She was tense all right, but not at all scared, like I would of thought. She didn't look so much like a kid from the Nebraska cornfields, but as if she'd been around a long time. When she unzippered, though, she was beautiful. Her zippers worked silently, as if they'd been oiled. The only sound she made was of somebody holding their breath.

I was trembling all over, and I thanked my stars for that strong right arm so she didn't have to help me on to the bed or anything.

She didn't do much talking at first, but afterwards she told me about what happened in Nebraska and how she wanted to get off the Street. If she could just make it fast enough, she said, she would open a little restaurant in Las Vegas and be set for life.

At first I was just looking at her, I hardly heard a word she said. It was that good to see a thing so perfect. Her skin was almost bronze, with two wider circles of light above where her clothes evidently filtered the sun. The notion crossed my mind as I squatted there, keeping myself covered, that she was just like those cornfields she came from, full of silk hair and golden light. Only her using herself like that was like shucking the leaves back to find the corn was ruined.

Maybe it was thinking crazy thoughts like that that triggered it off, but all of a sudden we started hating each other. I have thought it out over and over, but still I cannot remember what started it. Maybe it was not really thinking about cornfields at all; maybe it was Amy and her ill-timed visit. Because while Amy had been telling me about my strong hand and how I could lift her to the ceiling, I'd had a sort of pain in my chest, exactly at the curve of the bone—how shall I say it?—a "sorrow." I guess that's what love is, and all the stories about happy love are a fake. It was too bad that the thing, whatever it was, had to grow in me just that time La Sylphe was there.

And so there was La Sylphe lying there with one arm behind her head, I could see she enjoyed letting me look at her, and her greedy fingers playing with the money I'd made in my own little hell. I felt she was flaunting herself, that she wanted me to feel my ugliness. And I started thinking what a stupid animal she was living that way when she had a body that was as near perfect as a body can be. I guess I started thinking of what a person can do if he's born with two arms and two legs just like everybody else. So I hated her as if she were some sort of scab on the face of the earth, deforming it. It was as if her kind of ugliness only made mine worse.

So I must have been the one who said the first word, maybe wanting to get even with her for using herself like garbage. Then she lashed into me. She said I stank, that all cripples stank, that they never washed, and if there was anything in this world that made her sick to look at it was a cripple. She spat on the floor and said if I ever told anyone she'd been there, she'd have her man, Batchelli, tear me to pieces.

I just sat in the middle of the bed till she was through. Then I jeered at her for saying cripples stank. I said she was capable of any filth for money and she knew it. She screamed at me that there wasn't enough money in the world to make her look at me again.

She had the door open, and at that moment it was worth all I had to get her back, to humiliate her. I named a fantastic figure, so much money that I felt myself grow cold I was so scared at what I'd said, even though I still had more, and at the same time the "sorrow" seemed to burst in my chest, it hurt so bad. But I had the satisfaction of seeing her stop short, her back up against the wall, like her legs had turned weak.

"You don't have it," she said, drawing in her breath.

I knew that to remove the pipe in front of her would be a dead giveaway. But at that moment I hated her more than I loved money. It was like a revelation, almost like a conversion, that you could feel that deep about anything. Just then money was my only weapon against her, but it made me stronger than she was. Because when she saw that coil of money rolled tight as tape she dropped her purse down on the chair. And it was as I'd said: she was capable of anything for money. Only this time there was absolute silence, like we were digging a grave. And I'll never forget the look on her face when she saw the money. It was the look of a murderer, a madman, who sees you have food in your hand and he's starving. His first impulse is to kill you and tear the stuff out of your hands, but he has to pretend to be sane long enough to get near you .... I ought to have known by that look that I should have cleared out of Dauphine Street that night. Because the next night she and a couple of her boys broke open my lock, took every dollar and set fire to the bed.

I have not seen La Sylphe in the Quarter since then, so maybe she made it to Las Vegas after all. But several people have told me they've seen her around, that Batchilli beat her and left her for dead, taking all the money.

But it was strange what happened afterwards. I never said a word to anybody about it, so I don't know how it got around. Maybe La Sylphe herself told it. Anyway, it got around the Quarter, and guys who'd never talked to me before began asking me for a match and the first thing I knew they'd be talking to me about La Sylphe. It was like they were just waiting for a chance to talk.

I have moved to a better place, with heat all winter. I still have my spot on the Street, and I do pretty good, but somehow I don't save much. I don't cook anymore, it's too lonely eating in my room. So I go to Holmes' now and then; a bunch of us guys have got the habit of eating there. And I am buying a La Scala accordion, the best; you can play it pretty good with one hand.

CHEAPER POTATOES

Back in the Thirties, Wing had left Becky in Silver Valley and gone, like his grandson today, to look for work in Seattle and Alaska. Wing had thought then it'd be only a temporary thing: they'd be mining again soon at the C & L Silver-Lead & Zinc Company. He was young and strong, and when he'd kissed Becky as she'd followed him out to the bus carrying Franklin in her arms—Ephraim had stayed in school that day as they hadn't wanted him to miss any more days—Wing had settled himself in his seat, looking out at her and the baby named for the new President.

Either he'd be back by Christmas, Wing said, or he'd get a permanent job and send for her. There was no way for Becky to wipe the tears from her face because she was holding Franklin up so that he could see his Daddy, so she had stood there outside the bus window, the tears rolling down onto the baby's shirt until, after an unbearable moment of indecision when it had seemed impossible to Wing that he could actually be going to leave her, that he must get off the bus and take his family home and put Franklin to bed in his crib and then he and Becky and Ephraim would eat spaghetti with powdered milk again for supper (but no matter, they'd be together), until the bus growled, Becky turned her head away in resignation and courage, Franklin began to cry, and the moment had passed: Wing was headed due West.

The distances that stretched longer and longer between him and Becky had caused a sickness to grow in his stomach, but it was a plain fact that a grown man with a family had no time to be homesick, he had a job to do, which was: to find a job—the rest would be easy. So he hoarded his money and whenever the bus stopped he drank water instead of Coca-Cola, figuring every five nickels he saved would accumulate a day's grace: there were still plenty of places a man could get a whole meal for two bits.

It was already late afternoon by the time they arrived in Seattle and Wing stood in the station a little dazed: he had hoped they'd make better time. He'd wanted to be able to check out a couple of fishermen's coves before dark, and now here it was nearly four o'clock, he'd have to find a place to flop, but he knew himself not to be the flophouse kind: he wasn't ready to bed down with bedbugs and winos. There was a Salvation Army not far away, but he didn't feel sufficiently Down-and-Out for that kind of charity either. Hell, he'd just *arrived*, he wasn't looking for a handout, there were probably guys who needed it more than he did, old guys who maybe wouldn't ever again have a chance to land anything: he saw them now, panhandling, asking *him* for a handout. Resolutely, Wing shook his head.

Still it was a new place, therefore a place of hope, and he knew himself to be capable of anything. He'd hardly been sick in his life, he'd shovelled tons of rock a day, he'd helped carve out the mines of Silver Valley from the bowels of the earth, down to where China was supposed to be and back.

A fellow by the name of Emmett Kearney, an old guy he'd talked to on the bus, was now trailing out of the station after him. Wing wasn't sure he wanted him around, though Kearney seemed a harmless enough old geezer. His jacket was as dirty as if he'd been camping out in it, but his face, at least, was not umbered by gallons of cheap wine, and his eyes were as bright as a trout's scales. Still you had to be careful.

Wing was trying to look as if he knew his way around the city, so he announced: "Thought I'd check out Third and Fourth Avenues. Get an idea of what's been going down. Too late, I'd guess, to go to the employment offices." Wing controlled his tone so that it became a statement, not a question: he didn't want Kearney to think he was inviting suggestions.

Kearney shrugged. "Every day they write up any jobs they got on their blackboards. It's on a first-come, first-served basis: that means if you wait up all night maybe you get an address so you can follow up a lead. When you get there, you find out that maybe five hundred other guys have found out about this same lead. Anyway, you've spent your carfare following the lead, so you fill out the form. They take it and say they'll let you know if there's a fish run or maybe a sawmill going to cut up some logs. But who needs lumber?" Kearney pointed vaguely. "There's mountains of lumber piling up, rotting in the sheds. You got a place to stay?" Kearney added abruptly. "In case they want to get in touch?"

For a moment Wing considered making up an address, he didn't want to listen to the old man, he didn't want to hear any doom and gloom, he *had* to believe he was meant to be lucky, that unlike tens of thousands he'd get a job here. Faith in yourself was like working in the hardrock, you lived by it: but you could have a rockburst that could crush you.

"What kind of work you trying to get?" Kearney pursued when Wing didn't answer.

"Miner. Hardrock."

"Not much mining going on around *here*," observed Kearney drily. "Mostly—when they have it—it's fishing and timber. But ships now are just kept in anchor, rusting out. Doesn't pay them to make a run."

Wing tried to sound both good natured and reasonable about it: "Looks like people would be eating fish nowadays. Maybe they don't need metal out of the mines, but they got to *eat*!" he exclaimed with as much heartiness as he could muster.

Kearney was staring at him in brooding silence as if Wing were some Chinaman who'd just come off the boat and if Wing could speak the lingo Kearney would tell him all about it, and what Kearney would say was: 'Go back to your rice paddy lickety-split.' "Where'd you get *that* idea?" said Kearney at last. "That they got to eat?" Kearney began moving away. *At least he knows where he's going.* "Well *I* got to eat," said Wing in a conciliatory tone, "and you too. If you like—I got a couple of sandwiches left ...." He pulled out what remained of the sandwiches Becky had packed for him and showed them to Kearney. *Well you'd think I was showing him the Comstock Lode*, thought Wing and felt ashamed of his generosity, it was such a meager thing.

"I got a better idea. Hold up on those ... just put em right back in your pocket and come with me. I got a place ...."

They walked past the nailed-shut stores on Third Avenue and proceeded south of Yesler Way by way of a route that was obviously clear to Kearney, but was an endless maze to Wing. "Hey," Wing tried to joke. "This is worse than being down in the mine: we at least got tunnels!" Once or twice as their path seemed more and more isolated, suspicion gripped him: maybe this guy was leading him into a trap where Wing would be robbed and thrown from a pier. He began to imagine his body bumping up against the pilings like rotting driftwood, imagined Becky waiting for him ....

What he could not have imagined was what they came to: a city of discarded old men.

"How you like this?" asked Kearney, as dusk was descending on the city within a city. Wing, who'd grown up not far from the Snake River, within perpetual sight of the blue Minodkas, stared at the makeshift shacks with shock and dismay: *Nothing but bums and bindlestiffs. Did I come all the way here just to drydock with these losers?* Kearney led him to his own shack, nailed together from sheets of tin which were already curled and rusting at the edges. He and Kearney bowed their head to enter the door, across which Kearney had nailed a sort of ragged poncho. Inside, Wing saw a couple of empty milk crates and a pair of mattresses—"One to sleep on, and one for a blanket," joked Kearney. Unlike the other shacks, Kearney had covered the ground with broken pieces of slate picked up from wrecking-ball sites. Kearney showed him how well insulated the shack was. "You'd be surprised how warm we keep here." He banged on the walls of the structure to show how firm they were: "See that? Two layers of newspaper, one of cardboard. I'm thinking of getting the walls painted soon as I can find a can of paint left out somewhere .... Something lively: we got a guy from Detroit here, he's a good artist. I may get him to do me some artwork. Fact is, we got a lot of talent here, a lot of talent. We're not just ..." his words wandered off into the evening air. He offered to show Wing around, introduce him to his pals. Wing demurred, saying he didn't want to trouble anybody. Actually, he was trying to dissociate himself from the place, he didn't want Kearney to think he was going to stay in the camp for any time at all: tomorrow, Wing thought he'd push on, he'd land something, maybe find a fishing boat anchored in some quiet cove, just waiting for somebody like Wing to bring him good luck on a run. But he didn't brag to Kearney about what he might do tomorrow, he had the feeling that everything Wing wanted to say, Kearney had already heard, and Wing didn't want his own illusions shattered, he wasn't going to let these guys talk him out of his future.

"Let's get some wood and build us a fire," said Kearney. "Make some coffee for the sandwiches. But first maybe I ought to show you the toilet—"

Wing, dazed and shaken, found himself following Kearney around, asking questions: it was a role he detested—he was accustomed to telling other guys what to do in the mine. But he was on alien turf and he allowed himself to be led like a greenhorn as they walked toward the beach.

Overhead the evening sky was filled up with veins of silver, clusters of ore gathering around dark-blue pockets. Wing wished himself a mile underground; he would have preferred a forty-pound jackhammer tearing at his shoulder to this, walking out on the beach to take a piss. He and Kearney made their way over makeshift pontoons of rotting lumber and rusting metal to the wooden outhouses. As they approached, even the salt fresh air could not cover the stench. Wing groaned his humiliation: but to his surprise the beach was astonishingly clean. The ocean winds blew away most of the flies, and the men searching endlessly for trash or driftwood to keep their fires going left the sand clean if deserted-looking.

They found two friends of Kearney's waiting for them when they got back. Kearney introduced them as Hackett and Grogan.

"Seen you brought a newcomer," said Hackett. "Thought we'd ask, can he help build a coffin?"

"A what?" gasped Wing. "I'm a miner, not a carpenter."

"You don't need to know nothin about carpentry to build a coffin," Hackett assured him. "Nothin but a box."

"Yeah," added Grogan, "and if it don't fit too good—no problem."

"Whose coffin?" Kearney asked. "Who died?" Wing realized from the question that Kearney had been away for some time.

"The red head." said Hackett. "Guess you knew him better than I did. The one used to work in the lumber camps. The one said he used to be a friend of Anna Louise Strong. Of course every Wobblie around here," he added to Wing, "says he used to be a friend of Anna Louise Strong. But *I'm* the only one who ever saw her, I'll bet you. Saw her talkin to Lincoln Stephens one time. I used to deliver stuff to that newspaper she worked for, the one really got her into all that trouble, *The Call*—"

"What about Red?" interrupted Kearney. "What are they going to do about burying him? Did he have any kin?"

"No, no kin at all. But a bunch of us oldtimers want to have a kind of reunion. We figure we got at least thirty bonny fide used-to-be I WW's in this here camp alone. We gonna give him a regular send-off. Get some of the old guys who were in the Nestor Building when they wrecked the office. Play taps, sort of. Anyway," —addressing Wing— "if you could lend us a hand? Even though you *not* in the carpenters' union."

Kearney objected. "You're already asking this man to give you some of his time. And we haven't had supper yet. We're going to eat soon as we get this fire going."

The men immediately offered to share their day's assets: Grogan, who had a paper permit allowing him to use the breadline, pulled out what was left of his lunch; Hackett claimed to have saved out what a housewife gave him while he was door-to-dooring that morning; but the contents of the stained bag he pulled from the pocket of his blue canvas jacket, on which Wing made out the faded black letters HOSPITAL, had the look of leftovers from a patient's tray, complete with paper napkin: nobody in the camp would have spent a nickel on paper napkins.

They sat around the fire exchanging stories. Kearney had built an excellent fire in a trashcan, leaving ventholes for the smoke to escape. They fed the blaze with dried driftwood, boards of rotting lumber or pieces of coal Grogan had collected along the railroad ties.

"What happened to Red?" asked Kearney. "When I left he was on the wagon. He couldn't take a drink without it making him sick as a dog. He should have gone into the hospital: You can't cure an ulcer on booze."

"Don't any of us know exactly what *did* happen. He was sick, he was drinking too much, as much as he could get, and I guess he started bleeding."

"The hospital finished him off, you know that!" exclaimed Grogan with contempt. "He should never have let them take him to the hospital."

"Well," observed Hackett, trying to mollify him. "You pick up a man in the street, he's about to die of pneumonia out there, he's not about to complain about what you do with him. They found him on Washington Street. They thought he was drunk, but he'd probably just fainted. His ulcer was bleeding him to death."

"Well, what then?" Angrily Kearney shoved a piece of wood into the trash can, which began burning more quickly than he wanted it to, so he tried to snatch it back from the fire. The hot ashes blew onto his shaggy jacket and he began brushing them off, cursing furiously: "Damn it all to hell, can't even find a decent piece of firewood anymore, and all that stuff rotting, rotting rotting in the yards. I'm going to *rustle* me some lumber pretty soon, they don't watch out ...."

Grogan shrugged. "Yeah, then you'll be warm enough. They'll lock you up till this here Depression is over and done with, till *you're* over and done with." Kearney glowered at him, his silence acknowledging the truth of what Grogan said. "Anyway, are you listening to us or you going to burn yourself *up* tryin to keep warm? They picked up Red on Washington Street, and that's all we know. There wasn't a *thing* wrong with his heart, he only had this itty-bitty ulcer—"

"What you mean itty-bitty? He was hemorrhaging," contradicted Hackett. "Listen, Grogan, you got to stop being one of these persecution nuts. They've stopped shooting down Wobblies, you know. They don't give a damn about us anymore, cause we're all dying like rats anyway."

Grogan remained surly. "You'll never convince *me* they didn't black bottle him."

"What's that?" Wing felt obliged to ask, though he didn't want to listen to the answer. He was trying to concentrate his efforts on what he would do tomorrow. But the fire, the hot coffee, and the aimless, ricocheting conversation, along with the strange futureless society in which he found himself—a society without hope, responsibility or higher aim than to get through the day—had paralyzed his will. It was as if he were caught up in a dream where all the scenes and talk were out of his control; but at least, however terrifying the events, he need feel no guilt about them: he need only lie there and listen or force himself awake.

"Kearney," Grogan was saying, his voice rough with bitterness. "Explain it to this guy, what a black bottle is."

"I don't know what it is, I only know what they *say* it is."

"Well then, say what they say it is!" exclaimed Grogan fiercely.

"*Who* says?" Wing felt suddenly exhausted. He thought with deep grief and longing of Becky and the kids.

Kearney slapped the soot from his hands. "The men here say, especially the older guys who were here during the General Strike, they say They're trying to get rid of us all. That They don't want us or need us anymore, and as soon as They get the chance—the old men say— They're gonna poison us off ...."

"For Chrissake, who says that? You guys gotta all be crazy here ...." Wing half rose to his feet, as if he were going to leave them, but no one took the slightest notice. He squatted down again on his heels close to the fire.

"It's those damned interns, they don't care about you. If they don't actually poison you (which *I'm* not saying they *don't*)," added Grogan, "they sure as hell don't encourage you to take up your bed and walk. They'll bury you there—bed right on top of you."

"And what's this new guy doin here? You bring him?" asked Grogan abruptly of Kearney, as though Wing were deaf and dumb and couldn't speak for himself.

"Lookin for work," said Kearney, glancing in sad apology at Wing.

"And you said that with a straight face too, didya? Hee hee hee," nickered Grogan, looking up at the sky while taking out his sack of Durham. Curving a piece of wrapping paper cut down to size, he shook the tobacco in as into a chute. "Smoke?" he offered Wing in a dour but conciliatory way.

Wing shook his head. "Never took it up. A smoker in the mines is more dangerous than dynamite, cause you're apt to be more careless with it."

"So you're a miner. And what do you think of the Industrial Workers of the World?"

The phrase detonated around Wing's head: *aw, these guys are just a bunch of reds. Should of known that.* He weighed his words before answering. He didn't want to alienate these men. "I'm for the WFM. Guess people like to fight for theirselves right? Like the auto workers, the garment workers, you know? I just don't see how you guys can believe there could be *one* union for everybody."

"You'll find how there can be—when you get hungry enough," Grogan said. "What do you think you're sittin on your ass for right now, except you're already in the Big Union—the International Union of the Unemployed."

"What about that National Recovery Act that's gonna let everybody organize?" intervened Kearney with an air of compromise.

"Recovery! Sounds like a hospital ward to me! We're not going to recover from this till they figure out what to do with fourteen million people with nothin to do. And you know how they're gonna do that?"

Wing said he didn't know.

"Well, you'll find that out too. You got any kids—boys? *You'll* find out."

Suddenly they all became gloomy; they were all men separated from their families. Grogan said he hadn't seen his wife in over a year. "But I'm gonna go back East for Christmas if I got to ride the rods." One by one the men began taking out their worn wallets and exchanging snapshots of their children, their wives. Some showed cards from employers who had asked them to call back in a week or two: the cards were mottled with small black mold spots from the rain and fog of Seattle.

The exchange of snapshots had cast a despairing mood over them all. They began to knock out the fire, saving out any half-burnt pieces of wood for morning. Grogan seemed to repent of his manner toward Wing long enough to give him some advice. "Nothin here in Seattle, boy. If there's anything left to get, it's up in the North country. You can take a ferry and be there in a few days. I mean, if you got money to *get* there ...."

* * * * *

49

The following morning he and Kearney rose early: they didn't stop to make a fire but ate a cold breakfast in the shack. Kearney gave him some directions and a few warnings—not everybody could be trusted, he added, looking away. Kearney said he was reluctant to pass judgment on the rest of the world, but he knew for a fact that one man in the camp had been robbed and cast into the sea after winning a pile at a card game. So if Wing had any money, he should sew it up good in the lining of his pants or his shirt.

Before starting out for the employment agencies Wing asked if he could borrow one of Kearney's books that looked to him to be pretty interesting. He might read it, he said while waiting around for an interview. "*Interview*?" echoed Kearney, shrugging as at some childish fantasy.

Wing hesitated: his question seemed, even to himself, ridiculous. "What kind of address do you think I should write down? General Delivery?"

"No need to do that. Anything you have sent here, the postman knows me. We got an Unemployed Citizens' League that helps keep us honest. We got a vigilante committee, a mail committee, a food distribution committee, they handle all the stuff from the city relief, and a sanitation committee—keeps guys from pissin in the ocean—-You're welcome to stay here long as you want, Wing," Kearney suddenly interrupted himself. "But my advice would be the same as Grogan's. This is a city of old men."

"Aw come off it, Emmett. You're not even fifty."

Kearney stared at him with a bitterness so deep that his voice did not even show any emotion: "You don't think fifty is old?" After a moment he handed Wing a fat book bound in red and black. Wing weighed it in one hand, considering whether he wanted to tote such a heavy book around with him. "An atlas, is it? Any good maps?" Wing flipped it open.

"A novel."

"Oh, a novel," said Wing, losing interest. "I never read that kind of romantic stuff. Just give me a good plain horsethief anytime. You got a Zane Grey?"

After a week in Seattle, Wing had to admit Grogan and Kearney were right; there was no work for miners. Nor for carpenters, plumbers, fishermen, or professors. The morning he stood in line with a Doctor of Philosophy who was trying to get a job in an unemployment agency writing job resumes for the unemployed, Wing decided to risk all and take the ferry to Anchorage. But it would be turning cold fast and Kearney warned him that if he was going to try the last frontier, he'd better hustle: he'd freeze his ass off if he got there in the dead of winter. He looked down with a strange mixture of pity and contempt at Wing's jeans, rubbed thin at the knees. "Goddam, Wing, we'll find you some warm clothes before you go." True to his word, Kearney went around the camp, bartering coffee, cigarettes, and some commissary-issued cans of lard in exchange for a pair of old rubber boots and a coat many sizes too big for Wing: it fell right down to his ankles. Kearney comforted him: "Under that big coat you can wear whatever else you got: you can sleep in it if you need to. A big coat with plenty of pockets is all a man needs in this world." Kearney almost grinned: he told Wing a story of a man who'd camped out on the park bench for weeks, everything in his coat pockets, till the police found him one morning drunk and froze-to-death. "It's not being hungry that kills you, it's drinking to keep from *thinking* that gets you in the end," added Kearney philosophically. "Here—have another Zane Grey—a gift from us folks back home."

They walked together to the Sound, where Kearney stood with his pipe in his hand, like a small flag a patriotic child might carry to a ship's christening. Now and then Kearney would raise the pipe in the air and nod encouragingly. Wing could taste the fear in his mouth as he waved goodbye to Emmett, drifting farther away than ever from home and the land he knew: the ferry was soon navigating through the gleaming water of the Sound, and Wing (like some Gold Rush miner, he thought), was heading for the last frontier.

It was a cold, miserable trip, there was hardly anyone for Wing to talk to: apparently folks had given up rushing up to the Northernmost flank of the country for jobs. They were hunkering down where they were born, hanging on to local identifications that might qualify them for relief. A migrant like himself, Wing considered ruefully, was sure to be feared and detested, since it was plain as day that he came to take work that might be given to one of the local folks; or else, failing to find work, he was in their eyes just another vagrant: than which nothing was held in greater suspicion by folks raised on thrift and providence.

It had begun to rain almost the moment he set foot on board, and afterwards it was his invincible belief that it rained all the way from Seattle to Alaska. The few fishermen on board who were also headed North were glum and uncommunicative. He saw no women except a couple of young girls from whom Becky would have averted her eyes: they were naked to the hams and painted to the eyelids. They seemed to be making a little money on board—god knew where they took the men they disappeared with from time to time. There was one other passenger on board, who looked to Wing to be one of your "pink shirt" gamblers: he claimed to be playing for pennies, but every now and then Wing noticed green money going under the table. Wing touched-for-luck the few bucks he had sewn into his red flannel shirt. He swore to himself not to take the shirt off until it was padded thick as a quilt with money.

But his biggest problem at the moment was keeping warm; even with the long coat Kearney had got him, he felt frozen to the bone; obviously they were not going to waste heat on a few die-hard fishermen and a couple of chippies: so Wing paced up and down, going out on deck when the wind was not coming directly down from the Arctic. He began a letter to Becky, but he didn't know whether he'd have the courage to send it—he was so ashamed of his handwriting. Damn it all, if only his folks could have sent him to Boise to school. But there was no sense in complaining, he was a hell of a lot better off than *they* had been: homesteading, cutting down the everlasting sagebrush, fighting the black volcanic rock, planting potatoes and beans and corn with no fences to keep out the ranging cattle. They hadn't even had screens in their windows during those first years on the land: every day his poor-sainted-Mother would spend a half-hour before dinner killing flies so the men could sit down to eat a meal without being buzzed to Perdition.

Settling into a sheltered corner of the deck, Wing tried to find comfort in the fact that he, at least, had a neat little house back home in Silver Valley, which he partly owned, and which he was hellbent not to lose to the banks; and he had two terrific sons, smart as two whips, and a wife who'd never once crossed him in his life, and was right now maybe needing him: so what was there for *him* to do but stand up and be counted? Carefully he constructed word after word of his letter to Becky, adorning the big capital letters with graceful flourishes, and altogether admiring his own handiwork so much he almost forgot that he was near froze-to-death, had only a few bucks in his pocket, and that only God knew how he'd make it back to Silver Valley: if he failed, he might as well cut bait and run forever, Becky would go on welfare, and maybe be better off without him. But he wasn't going to fail, he was going to Do It. At that moment, surrounded by fjords and mountains and forests of firs as dense as the day of Creation, Wing vowed he would beat the odds or die.

When at last the ferry docked at Anchorage, Wing lost no time in looking around for a flophouse or Salvation Army: he headed straight for the beach where he rightly guessed there'd be another tent city, not as big as the one "Back Outside" as they called the States up here, but sufficiently crude and open as to let a young man like Wing try his luck with the rest of them.

But as soon as he laid his eyes on the place Wing became wary: these were a different breed of men—Last Chance hoboes, ready to steal your blanket while you slept, and leave you to freeze. When Wing arrived, nobody spoke to him. He was relieved, at least, that they didn't exchange conspiratorial glances, that it didn't suddenly occur to them that by joining together they could finish Wing off in a minute and bury him in the snow till Spring. Diffidently, Wing placed a tightly-rolled newspaper into the fire. Nobody thanked him or acknowledged his presence. He wanted to ask if it were possible to bed down somewhere in the camp, but he was scared to: bed down with whom? He wouldn't want to sleep under the same roof with any of these guys. Wing decided that the next best thing, for the moment at least, was to find some public building—a post office or hospital or even a bank—where he could warm up without worrying about who might put a knife in his back. So assuming a harmless, indecisive manner, Wing began backing away from the fire: unlike the well-built fire Kearney had so carefully tended, here they indifferently tossed whatever refuse they had handy. As Wing turned away, the dark smoke billowed toward the limestone skies.

There was still plenty of daylight left, so Wing was not feeling as anxious as he might have felt back home that the darkening wilderness might isolate him before he'd found shelter. But he was colder than he'd ever been in his life and he saw no so-called public buildings. He did spot what appeared to be a cheap sort of lunchroom with steamed-up windows: it had to be warm in there.

Wing sat down at the counter and asked for an order of fried potatoes: they'd be cheap but hot and would keep his belly feeling full till his luck improved. But when the potatoes were set in front of him, he was disappointed: they were cottage fries, mealy and greasy. But at least they were hot, that was all that mattered. He began eating slowly, letting the heat of the place warm him up. As he ate he thought about the potato, what a plague or godsend it could be. As a child back home in southern Idaho, he could remember a sea of potatoes extending across his parents' homestead. When it came time to harvest, every man, woman and child would be bent to the ground. And always, it seemed, they were rescuing the potatoes: from the late blight or the first killing frost or before they became nearly worthless on the market—farmers in Idaho were getting forty-five cents for a hundred pound sack that folks in Chicago would pay six-fifty for—he and his father had once stood beside a veritable mountain of potatoes, enough potatoes to feed a regiment through the entire First World War. But it hadn't paid to ship them, so they'd been left on the ground to rust and sprout ....

... Potatoes ... with their milk-eyed sprouts that sacrificed themselves like saints and grew to a greater blessing. That could be baked or scalloped or creamed or mashed or made into a cold vichyssoise fit for a Prince, or a hot soup fragrant with parsley and a squirt of lemon—a soup that could warm you to the bone, better than brandy it was for giving you joy without hunger. And even the raw potato, it too was a blessing: it could cure a cold, excite women, bring the rheumatism from out of your knuckles; its frothy enzyme could wear away a wart. The very skins held a secret power, full of the good growing stuff you needed to keep your teeth from falling out, while within the brown green or purple sacs were stored up all that protein needed for hungry schoolkids: like Abe Lincoln who'd warmed his hands on the way to school with the benevolent potato, then warmed his belly with it at lunchtime .... Goddam, potatoes BREATHED. They could change the temperature in your storage bin. And like humans, they could sicken and die, the rot smelling worse than a corpse. Not even formaldahyde-dipping could cure them of the cancerous black rot: he'd seen his mother scrub her hands over and over trying to wash out an

odor as strong as ether.

The tasteless lunchroom potato had made him homesick—not for Becky and the kids but for his own childhood home. Lord, *that* was a wilderness—a sagebrush wilderness, without trees: he hadn't even seen a tree till they made that trip to Salt Lake City. And then the miles and miles of sagebrush that it'd been his job to cut down for firewood; what a blaze it'd make: one big firecracker and you were right back to chopping the brush. That insatiable pot-bellied stove would devour all his hard labor at one gulp .... But he'd kept the fire going, Wing had. With temperatures at forty below to have let the fire go out would have spelled a quick hypothermal death; or to have let the red-hot iron belly of the stove crack from overheating; or to have failed to adjust the damper before going to sleep could also have meant death. And to have fallen into the Canal while getting those endless buckets of water for the potato fields might also have meant death. And bringing in the hay for seventy-two hours like his brother had once done might also have meant death. And walking to the one-room schoolhouse in a snowstorm might well have meant death. And going up to Silver Valley to work in the mines, having received all the booklearning he was to get in this life, without his folks, living in a boarding house alone while he worked a man's shift in the mines from the time he was sixteen, that also might have meant death.

But it was obvious that God had meant that Ephraim Wingfield should survive. Because here he was now, eating potatoes in a joint where it looked like possibly they still spit on the floor....At this moment Wing slid the last piece of potato into his mouth: it was quite cold now, but he savored it nonetheless, sweet to the taste as an after dinner creme de menthe. Feeling more cheerful and reconciled—his reverie on his folks' homesteading days had somehow given him new courage and an almost patriotic sense of his heritage—Wing moved toward the cashier at her register singing softly:

> Potatoes are cheaper
> Tomatoes are cheaper
> Now's the time to fa—a—ll ... in love.

A pretty woman, Wing was thinking.

"Fifty cents," she said.

He glanced quickly around the walls for a price list in order to correct this error. "Whaddye mean, fifty cents? All I had was an order of fried potatoes."

The cashier glanced over her shoulder toward the kitchen. She raised her voice slightly. "Fifty cents. You ate em, you pay for em."

"But how can that be?"

No one had even brought him a bill.

"A *miracle*," she said. "Every day of the year we got miracles here. Guys come in, they eat, and they *pay*."

"I never paid half a buck for an order of fried potatoes in my whole life. I could buy a whole hundred pound sack for that kind of money."

"Yeah? Well, I guess you got a whole new life ahead of you. You better pay now, this ain't the Salvation Army."

Wing looked around him for somebody to complain to about this outrage. But there was only one elderly man in the restaurant who looked steadily down at his coffee: *not going to get involved*, he profile said, plain as day.

"I could of got a whole dinner for twenty cents." Wing had the humiliated feeling that he was just babbling.

"Yeah, where? Back in the Forty-eight? Well go get yourself one then. But in *this* country, you pay for these potatoes, and you pay fifty cents."

The cook, who also seemed to be the owner, now came out of the kitchen. *Big as a brown bear*, thought Wing. Ridiculously it made him think of an old refrain: *Snap your fingers honey, I declare .... It's a bear, it's a bear, it's a bear ....*

"This guy givin you a hard time?"

The cashier shrugged, tore out a sheet of red-lined paper from a checkbook, wrote 50¢ right in the center, looped and noosed it around several times with her black pencil, then stuck it on a nail and waited for whatever was going to happen to happen.

With maddening calm she asked: "Call the police?" It was clear to Wing that she had absolute faith in the huge hand which now touched hers assuringly.

"Yeah. Give him five seconds, then get the police."

"Hey wait a minute! I didn't say I wouldn't pay. I'll pay —" Wing hated the sound of his quavering voice.

"You fucking well better pay, or Mr. J. Edgar Hoover will be on your case in just five minutes!"

The goddam thief has a sense of humor, thought Wing bitterly as he laid two quarters down on the glass counter. He tried to keep his fingers from trembling with rage as he surrendered the price of a hundred pounds of potatoes. The cashier picked up the quarters one at a time, using her nails like tongs, and tossed them into the register where they made a bright clinking sound like horseshoes hitting a stake. Wing was now in such a hurry to leave these robbers—before he got mad enough to yell out some ugly insult that would set him up for an assault charge—that he went out leaving Becky's letter on the counter. He rushed back in again almost immediately for his letter, but the cashier said she'd never seen any such thing. Wing, however, spotted a corner of the opened envelope in the trash: fortunately he'd not been so crazy as to send Becky money in an envelope protected only by a U.S. postage stamp.

But he was taking no more chances—merely for the sake of keeping warm—on confrontations with the locals. He walked back to the bus terminal, determined to stay there all night: he'd have to pretend he was waiting for a bus. He inquired at the window about a round-trip fare to Fairbanks. "And how long do you think you'll be in Fairbanks?" asked the clerk, who seemed to be just trying to be helpful; but Wing had become distrustful of personal questions, and answered him evasively. "Well," the clerk said, "your problem will be coming back. You want a round-trip ticket and here it's not yet full winter. But in a few weeks we won't be running any more buses between here and Fairbanks: so how would you get back?" Wing replied that he thought he had something lined up, at least for the next couple of months. But just to be certain, he added, he'd try to phone the guy in Fairbanks before making that long trip. Every hour or so Wing got up from his seat in the bus station and dialed the number of the pay phone in front of him. This charade seemed to convince the clerk that Wing wasn't just another bum trying to spend the night in a warm place: he let Wing wait out the night there till he could call Fairbanks again in the morning. Wing dozed, one eye on the clock. As soon as dawn broke through the windows—a strange purple sort of dawn that seemed to intensify the cold rain falling ceaselessly—he hiked out to the canning factories without stopping to eat: he was almost the first man in line. The smell of coffee made him feel sick, he could feel the emptiness of his belly like a cold swamp. When a vendor came by hustling his hot watery coffee, Wing gambled another nickel for the sake of his future.

At about eight o'clock the employment office opened. The men waiting in line were all told the same thing: they were not hiring here, but there was guaranteed work on Kodiak Island .... Wing wanted to punch the guy in the face, but instead he laughed a short bitter laugh, like a barking dog. Raging with anxiety and anger, he and several other guys who'd waited in line hiked back to the pier and caught the next ferry out to the Island. Eighteen hours later Wing was down to his last buck, but he had a job.

But it was no Cozy Cannery. On the Island they worked with fish brought directly from the sea: cutting it and slicing it and bagging it and freezing it and shipping it to the *table d'hotes* of the world. Seven days a week for seven weeks Wing cut his way through thousands of pounds of flesh, most of it pale and pink as flamingoes; his heart began to palpitate irregularly from the bennies he took to keep himself awake on the double shift of sixteen hours, and by the time the weather had turned bitter cold so that it was becoming impossible for fishing boats to go out on a run, Wing was coughing up an oozy phlegm, iridescent as caviar, from a chronic bronchitis. For weeks everything he touched or wore or ate smelled of fish. At night he dreamt of fish, lying inert till he attacked them with his long-bladed knife; but as he hacked through their milk-white bones, the fish would suddenly come alive; its eyes would open as if it had been merely asleep, not dead, and opening its mouth, it would become a talking fish, a remonstrative, rebuking, cunning, wheedling fish, that always outsmarted him. Leaping from his clutch as he tried to grip its glistening body, it would swim across the conveyor belt, evading him, always evading him, so that every night he dreamed he'd lost his job due to his own incompetence, and would awake in anguish to the daylight that had scaled the walls of his roominghouse while he slept and had painted his room a soft pink salmon color.

In spite of everything, he stuck it out, he endured, he saved more than he spent until, when the seasonal lay-offs had begun, his shirt was solidly padded with money, and by the time he again boarded the ferry for Anchorage and Seattle—navigating through icy waters within sight of icebergs that had once seemed majestic to Wing but now were merely menacing—Wing had saved enough to hunker down in Silver Valley with Becky and the kids to make it through the longest Depression in history.

But before the ferry returned to Seattle, it stopped once more at Anchorage: and Wing knew he had a thing to do. He had worked like hell, hardly spending anything on himself; but after a few weeks he'd bought a heavy lumberman's jacket and a fur cap which covered his head to the eyebrows. He'd also let his beard grow thick and curling around his face. The beard and the fur cap seemed to expand his entire body size: he looked fifty pounds heavier. Then for the final effect he'd bought a pair of cheap sunglasses—even Becky wouldn't have recognized him, he thought. He checked the departure time for Seattle, synchronized his watch with the ferry's banjo clock, and walked into Anchorage. He headed straight for the joint where he'd paid the price of a hundred pound sack for one potato.

He had chosen the busy noon hour: the place was gratifyingly crowded. Wing sat down at one of the small tables beside the window. He ordered half a fried chicken and some fried potatoes. He saw that they were the same sort of potatoes he'd eaten weeks before: razor-thin, weighing altogether about two ounces. Slowly Wing ate one or two slices, concentrating intently. Then unobtrusively he slipped the chicken into a paper napkin and shoved it into one of his pockets. From another pocket he drew out a small package, fastidiously wrapped in tinfoil. He set the package on the table, unwrapped the tinfoil, and carefully slid the dead rat onto his plate. Then he stood up, cursing loudly. His chair overturned with such force that Wing saw with satisfaction that he'd cracked the window: *that'll bring in cold air like a flood in a mineshaft.* "Christamighty, it's a rat, a goddam rat!" he cried at the top of his voice. Gagging and heaving he rushed out of the restaurant. He stood for a few seconds at the curb, continuing to gag. *(Bigod, I should have been an actor, I missed my calling. They'll be talking about the fried rat in that clip-joint from now till kingdom come*

....)

He had it all timed down to the wire. Within ten minutes he'd run like hell back to the ferry, they were pushing away from the pier, and he was heading back to Seattle. He stood on board deck waving and waving to the vanishing shore as if he were leaving a thousand friends behind, shouting triumphantly, "*Goodbye Alaska, for now and forever!*"

A MAN CALLED MANUEL

The smell of the sea always alerted her: by then Catalina knew they were close enough to stop. With a great groan Basilio would turn the car into a truck stop or small cafe and announce that they would eat first. He would have the tires checked, the gas tank filled, then join the children in the booth. Massive and silent, he would divide up the five hamburgers and french fries and order a bottle of coke. He himself did not eat then, but would sit and watch. Shortly after, he would begin to tense up, the tattooed birds on his biceps would seem to stir: "Drink up," he would order, glaring at his watch as if somewhere behind its luminous glow lurked his lifelong enemy.

He seemed always angry with the other kids, though not with Catalina. She was his favorite, partly because she was pretty, but more importantly because he and his wife, Rosa, who usually worked with the crew, had seen right from the beginning how Catalina moved, quick as the wind, soundless and smooth, no gesture wasted.

The day they'd discovered her, Catalina had been sweeping her parents' shack, moving quietly but efficiently around the room as she swept out dust, dry leaves, a few fallen crickets .... Once, according to the way her parents then described it to Rosa and Basilio, an armadillo had burrowed his way under the house, and Catalina had at once struck him a quick blow with her broom handle, stunning him.

"Afraid of nothing, she is. And fast," her father observed to Basilio, who had turned to exchange glances with Rosa. Rosa nodded approvingly.

"So ... you move real quick?" Basilio questioned her. Catalina had merely nodded shyly, but also with pride. She knew she could outrun all the kids in their family, even Mateo who she sometimes imagined as having run all the way to the border, never stopping till he reached Chicago where, they said, he made money, a lot of money. She had always been this way, from her earliest memories, when crickets and chameleons had scampered away from her running feet long before she could speak and call out their names. She had simply taken the company of all these living things for granted, like that of Jorge and Ema and Leonor and Ciro and Mateo, as simply part of their household, of her life.

"How many kids you have?" Basilio had asked. Then, since Rosa had made a chuckling sound in her throat: "No, *naturalmente*, not you, I mean—*tu madre*." Then everyone had smiled.

"We are altogether, seven," Catalina had replied, glancing at her father for permission to answer these strangers who had driven down to their village. "But Mateo has gone to *el Norte*. To Chicago," she added as if this explained everything.

Basilio had at once allowed her parents an advance of fifty dollars on Catalina's work, assuring them that she would earn much more working in the Rio Grande Valley; and that once every month or so Catalina would return to visit, with more than enough money for them all. Her parents had nodded stoically at this, understanding what must be said: and at once Catalina had been introduced to the others in Basilio's crew who had been peering at her from the car—to Manuel, Felicia, Magdalena and Isabel.

Since that day, however, the crew had not returned to the village. At first Catalina had been homesick, thinking often of how her toes had traced footprints like fossils in the soft dust; of how on her last afternoon in the village, while she had stood at the well, a chameleon, its throat engorged, had leaped across the stone wall. Quick as a flash she had caught it, cupping it in both hands; but at the sight of its swollen, throbbing throat, she had let it go. Since then, again and again, she saw or dreamed she saw the gold, greening flash of its tail as it had disappeared into the dark of the well.

The Coke bottle had gone from hand to hand. Isabel now passed it to Manuel. "How far we now?" asked Manuel, scarcely glancing at the near-empty bottle.

Basilio gripped his hands together; it was a sign, as the children knew, that his patience was not to be tried today. Perhaps, Catalina thought, it was because he had the kids all to himself. He and Rosa had quarrelled, and Rosa had stayed in bed: as soon as it was light, the crew had set out for the border.

Catalina knew that he would not reply to Manuel's question: he never liked to tell them how far away they were from any other place. Sometimes the children grew restless in the car, and would begin to count the miles to the next town, then the miles to the border. Sometimes when Basilio and the crew stopped to eat, they would continue their arguments in the gas station or cafe. Basilio didn't like that. Catalina was surprised at Manuel's not having learned yet not to ask such questions.

"About an hour yet," Basilio said, looking not at Manuel, but at a spot in the wooden booth just above Manuel's head. "You finish that damned drink yet?" Manuel turned the bottle upside down to show there was nothing left. At once they all rose. As she was the eldest, Catalina quickly herded the three other girls into the toilets. Manuel followed Basilio and, through the pasteboard partition which separated the rest rooms, Catalina could hear the men urinating. Catalina could tell which was Manuel and which was Basilio just by the sound. She knew she should, instead, be instructing the girls, as Rosa would have done, how they must work ....

"... already her throat swelled with love and fear ...."

But she paused, cocking her head to listen as she heard Manuel complain softly: "I need me a watch too. I need to know the time, *en punto.*"

Silence …. Basilio doubtless too surprised by this request to be angry or sarcastic with Manuel who was demanding something he must feel he had a right to, like a man.

That Manuel was a man, Catalina knew. All the children slept in the same bed; and although she and Manuel were separated from each other by the others, only a few weeks ago he had waited till they were all asleep; then, coming around to her side of the bed, he had kneeled and whispered: *"Soy un hombre. Y tu?"* She had not been frightened of course. She knew him too well, and besides she had understood his question perfectly well, only she had been afraid they would awaken Rosa and Basilio in the other room. Still, she could easily have sneaked out and gone with Manuel to the front porch or even beyond, into the star-filled darkness where none but the crickets and moaning tree frogs would have heard: but she was not ready yet. She had work to do with Basilio and Rosa, and besides, how would she run quick-as-the-wind if she became first, engorged like the chameleon with love, then heavy with child like *la madre*? Her instinct was to deny Manuel, to keep things as they were ….

"Hah, a watch you want now….What else you think you need? You need a girl pretty soon too maybe? Maybe you think one of my crew? …"

Catalina's heart turned over with fear. How would Manuel reply? It was a challenge, no doubt of it …. There was silence, she heard Basilio clear his throat and spit into the bowl. Then Manuel explained: "I just want to help …. I need to see the time. Sometimes I don't see the clock so good. Because Rosa said—-"

"Never you min' what Rosa said. I'm the boss here."

"O.K. O.K."

Catalina could imagine Manuel's soft, defeated air, his dark eyes …. She bent over Isabel. "You *got* to learn to tie your shoes, Isabel. 'Else you'll trip one day, and that'll be bad luck for you."

She was thinking it was true, Manuel did not see so good. He'd had a cough with fever, his body had broken out in a rash, they'd put him for a while by himself, away from the other kids. And soon afterwards Catalina had seen him steal a lady's glasses which lay on the counter of a big department store. Catalina had seen him from the balcony as she'd glanced down. She had signalled him not to do it; such random acts were forbidden. But though he had glanced all around him, and looked straight at her, he had not recognized her. She understood now, that he was like old people, going a little more blind every day.

"And don't forget," she instructed the girls, "you must move fast, fast as the wind. Like me …." Quickly, Catalina slipped past the other girls who, recognizing the game, tried laughingly to catch her. But

Catalina sped past them out onto the sundazzled highway.

As they all climbed back into the car they rearranged themselves as they had been instructed. When Rosa was with them, it was easy: a cluster of small kids in the back—the girls wearing new shoes and their prettiest dresses—looking like any other family on their way to a day's shopping in the big city where the shopkeepers gathered up their coins like bread. But without Rosa they looked a little lost, as if there were too many of them. So Basilio moved Catalina to the front seat and told her to sit up straight, it maybe would make her look a little older. Manuel was to sit in the back "with the other kids." There was a hard but reassuring core of authority in Basilio's voice as he made these arrangements.

"Maybe they won't ask us nothin' anyways. They know we got to spend money." Adding what was for Basilio a rare burst of humor: "We got to do our Christmas shoppin' early, that's all." But when Isabel began to giggle, he hit her—though not hard—and told her to shut up and be ready.

The sun was high in the sky when they crossed over. The young man at the border had waved them on, scarcely bothering to check their trunk. Perhaps Basilio, not wishing any trouble today, had slipped him a *mordida*, or maybe he too worked for Basilio and Rosa, just like herself and the others. But more than likely (the clearness of her own mind astonished her today, maybe she was quickly becoming a woman after all, it was said to do things for your head), maybe the man was just hungry and not thinking right about his work, maybe like them, he had had a hamburger and french fries for breakfast long hours ago that morning.

Because (of course) it had been much longer than Basilio had said to Manuel. At least three, four hours, she guessed. But she would not question Basilio: he had said often enough that all they needed to know was that at the right moment they were to drop what they were doing and join him at the car.

She wondered whether they'd have another stop, or whether Basilio would want to push on, to get to the city. It was beginning to seem too short a day: where exactly had they lost time? Perhaps they had taken longer than she realized, talking in the restrooms ... or perhaps because of his quarrel with Rosa last night, Basilio had had a late start. Rosa had sulked and said she wouldn't go with him to the city, that he could go without her—though, of course, she'd added, goading him, without her he'd return with nothing worthwhile: he had no taste, no judgment, she'd said. Basilio had hit her for that, a resounding crack, like a tree limb snapping in the wind .... Catalina now glanced nervously over her shoulder at Manuel, who either could not see her anxious look, or was pretending not to see. For the first time, an uneasiness constricted her throat. Not really fear; no, she was not afraid—she was only excited: she would surprise them all today.

As they turned into the city plaza, she saw by the clock in the tower of the County Building that it was 1:25.

"O.K. Check the time." Basilio pointed vaguely toward the clock in the tower. His words were breathy in a way Catalina had not heard before. "O.K?" This time it was a question, but he did not wait for a reply. "At two o'clock—you be back here. *En punto*!" he said, and waved them away.

Soundlessly as water into sand they flowed into the store. The three girls, Felicia, Magdalena, and Isabel, moved down one of the aisles together, then separated almost at once: they were headed for Coats & Sweaters. From the corner of her eye Catalina could see how well Isabel was following instructions: how languidly she pushed the dresses along a rack while her eyes roved with intense simulated boredom around the store. Magdalena went at once into the dressing room: only moments later Felicia followed her with an armful of dresses and two or three coats. Soon Isabel gave up guarding her corner of the store and—her arms also loaded with dresses—followed the other two into the dressing rooms. Catalina knew they would emerge one at a time, swollen like small pregnant animals. They would walk quickly but calmly to the front of the store, keeping always within sight of the big wall clock while they watched for the exact moment when Basilio would be starting his car. If necessary, they would make a run for it, straight from the dressing rooms, but Basilio always preferred a graceful exit: he didn't like, he said, to have to go driving like crazy through the city.

Quickly, Catalina sized up the store. They'd been here twice before: it was not like an expensive jewelry store. Here one had to choose more carefully, but she knew where the best things were kept. And no one bothered to look at her, an ordinary girl with straight black hair and brown legs, moving effortlessly through the store. The last time she had worked with Magdalena; this time she was on her own. She knew she was supposed to try for leather jackets, but she wanted to surprise them. She walked once at a reasonable pace all around the store—past suits, coats, boots, shoes, drapes, curtains, carpets, pillows, lamps, knitted baby clothes; past furniture of every kind—cribs, coffee tables, lamps, desks, beds; past electrical cooking equipment of every sort: to make ice cream with, to bake cakes with, to grind and extract and pound with, for broiling, baking, barbecuing ....

Ignoring all this with what she believed to be an air of terrific idleness, Catalina strolled to the glass counter where they kept some jewelry and a few watches—under glass, to be sure, but the case was not locked. The jewelry was not worth much, she knew, though some of it looked so much like real gold and real silver that for a moment Catalina paused and stared childishly at the rings and necklaces. But no, she was not going to be fooled. Only in the locked showcases of real jewelry stores (where, Rosa said, they would have been spotted in a minute by store detectives), did they keep any gold and silver worth being melted down .... *Not worth the risk*, had always been Rosa's warning. But Catalina now stood leaning against the glass case; she could feel suddenly how her own breath came and went, as if she had been running. A quick glance at the wall clock told her she had nearly ten minutes yet before Basilio would begin to race his motor: she would make another turn around the store, get a drink of water, and return.

This time she passed Manuel as they circled a fenced-in area, above which someone had nailed a sign: *Toy-joys on wheels.* The fence was broken through, the aisle was a clutter of tricycles, scooters, wagons, wheel barrows, skateboards. Propped up along the fence as though standing beside a real playground was a red bicycle. Catalina saw how Manuel glanced at the bicycle with longing, though it was far too small a bike for him, and the cheap paint was already scratched. Still, she thought as she saw how Manuel looked at it, how nice it would be to have one, to balance on the bar in front while Manuel drove her around and around the plaza. As he passed her, his eyes moved from the bicycle to her face, and it was as if the longing she had felt in his body had leaped to his eyes and the dark, dimming gaze now grew suddenly bright with love; so that her own heart spilled out toward him, like seed shaken in the wind.

She wished she could seize the bicycle for him; but of course they could never do that ... though she found herself imagining that, like a cowboy of old, Manuel could leap onto the bicycle, lift her in his arms, and instead of racing to Basilio's car, they would speed away together, hidden away forever in the great *Estados Unidos* .... But even while she dreamed this dream in a quick little explosion, Manuel passed her as though he had not recognized her, and she knew they could never do this. They would only be caught, disgraced, and sent back across the border. And once caught—finger-printed, identified—they could no longer work; in the future, the store detectives would recognize them at once, and Basilio might abandon them to the police—or even, as he sometimes threatened—to the highways. He could not run his business, he often said, with faces everybody knew.

So not the bicycle of course. But she would offer some gift to those sad eyes which had lit up with love like fireflies floating through the dark. When she had made her final turn around the store, she stopped at the display case under whose glass lay several watches. One of these she at once chose for Manuel—a watch whose glowing digits pulsed the seconds faster than she would have believed time could go .... The time she saw, was 1:55 *en punto.* Almost simultaneously, moving so fast she could barely see her own arm, Catalina reached out her hand for the watches. She was certain she had been both quick and deft; yet somehow the impact of her arm had unbalanced the showcase: as she turned to go, it tilted and came crashing down behind her.

Still, she was not yet afraid: rather, she at once geared her body for that agile speed in which she trusted. Pivoting slightly, she poised in mid-air like a dancer for a few seconds, then fled down the aisle toward the street entrance. She ran straight through the store, her feet skimming the floor; she ran past the clothing, the furniture, the household appliances, the toys and the bicycles, thinking to herself that she was not running, or even flying, but flowing—swept along in an invisible flood of love for Manuel, whose eyes she was already seeing light up with a new kind of vision, a vision of her love for him, as she offered him this gift—a gift that would allow him always to know the right hour to come running back to them .... to her.

But at her back had gathered a small crowd of people who were angry, very angry, in a way Catalina had never seen. They cried out that they knew her, they had seen her before. Why were they so angry? Catalina wondered; the watches were not theirs, yet they were furious all the same. Now they flowed into the street; they ran after her, lining the curb, where they watched and scolded and yelled at her. Perhaps they would pursue her all the way to the car where Basilio waited .... Not daring to look back for the others, for Magdalena, Felicia and Isabel, Catalina could only run, run as she had never run in her life, till she reached Basilio and the car. She at once hurled herself, breathless, into the back seat. Her chest ached with the awful certainty that everything had gone wrong. Tears of remorse filled her eyes as she saw that the people were surrounding—not Felicia, Magdalena, and Isabel, who had paused in their flight to look for Manuel—but Manuel. The people were cursing him, crying out with rage and contempt that he too was a *lobato*, a wolf-cub. They seized him and beat him with their handbags, their packages. At last a policeman came and grabbed Manuel by the collar, holding him far away from his own body, as though Manuel stank. Then he shook Manuel like a small wet cat.

Basilio yelled at the girls: "Goddam—get in the car!"

Catalina began to whimper.

"Shut up!" he hissed, turning his head only long enough to show her his clenched fist.

The three girls, panting with terror and relief, threw themselves into the car: they were safe. Basilio gunned the motor.

"Wait!" screamed Catalina. "Manuel is caught!"

"Son of a bitch," said Basilio, and took off like the howling wind through the city.

In the back seat Catalina sobbed, *Manuelito, Manuelito*, while the children patted her hand and tried to comfort her. "They gonna let him go," they murmured together like professional mourners. "They gonna let him go—"

"Hell, what happened with *you*?" Basilio interrupted with fury.

Catalina could only hold up the watches in explanation, realizing at the same moment that in her haste and confusion she had not even had time to hide the watches. "For Manuelito," she explained. "For his eyes—"

"Fuck his eyes!" exploded Basilio, glaring at the watches. "You *stupid*!"

Catalina began to sob hysterically. Lobato, *the people had called him*. Lobato. *Then the people knew who they were, Basilio and the crew, knew why they had come there: and knowing that, the angry people might never let Manuel go ....*

With a screech of tires Basilio suddenly turned off the highway, heading, as Catalina knew, for a bypass of the border check: it was used only for emergencies, as it was too easy to be cornered there—Basilio had used it only once before. Shaken with remorse, Catalina knew that it was her fault Basilio was now forced to use this bad road to get back, running the gauntlet with the crew. If they got back safe, it'd be a miracle, Basilio told them in a cold, furious voice.

Then abruptly he turned the car again, this time into a dirt road. It was barely more than a shallow pit, a gully, though it could be used as an access road to the highway.

"Get out," he ordered Catalina.

Catalina stared, her stomach churning with fear.

"Get out. We don't want you. We can't use you."

Catalina could not believe it, though she had been warned many times by Rosa. She had broken their law, she had endangered the safety of the crew: she had made herself, Manuel, and perhaps the others recognizable—to the stores, to the people, to the police.

"Get *out*," he repeated, raising his fist.

Catalina stopped sobbing and began to whimper softly; but she opened the door as she had been ordered to, and stood obediently in the road: *it was a test, a punishment; he did not mean it ... he could not mean it ....*

Basilio reached over and wrenched the watches from her hand. "Cheap junk ... Probably don't even run ...." Then with a lunge and a roar of the engine Basilio headed straight south with the crew.

For a moment Catalina stood in the road, stunned. Then in a flood of terror at this abandonment, she flung herself down, crying out and sobbing into the dust. It seemed to her she lay a long while sobbing, that she had lost sight of time altogether; yet when she raised her head from the dust she realized that she had for some moments become aware of a change in the sky, like a filtering down of the dark. Soon total darkness would come to the deserted road .... Still, she rested a while, listening to the cry of birds, the throb of cicadas, the hum of the city in the distance. Then she rose to her feet and began to walk very slowly in the direction of the city. After a few steps she stooped to remove her shoes; and gathering confidence from the familiar dust at her feet, she began to run. At first she ran awkwardly, then more confidently down the dusty road, till picking up speed and courage, she was soon running as fast as her legs could carry her toward the humming city: already her throat swelled with love and fear and the question she could hear herself asking—of the people, of the shopkeepers, of the police: *if they knew, if they could tell her, please, where is a man called Manuel?*

LOVE

Her sister Elisabeth had had a retarded child, whom she kept at home. There had never been any talk of his being sent to school. Elisabeth had named him Rolande, never dreaming of the dark tower that enveloped his intellect. When Rolande was big enough to lift his own heavy tricycle with ease from the front porch and down the steps to the sidewalk, and Elisabeth still had not succeeded in toilet training him or teaching him to hold a spoon, she had a nervous breakdown from which after a year she recovered, taking up her cross with tender anguish.

Rolande grew, playing happily outdoors, his legs at first spindly as a baby giraffe's, parted away from his body like some whimsical model of the eternal split between Body and Soul: always he smiled at his Aunt Julia, the face greeting her in guileless joy, while the feet dragged afterwards—a miscue, the face having entered before the rest of him.

Julia had watched him grow up, always feeling (certainly) pity— but also shame and sometimes fear, often finding herself praying silently, *Don't let it happen to me, dear God, don't let it happen to me.* At first Rolande was pleasant and pudgy, like a playful pet who never judged her, and who responded to her combing of his hair with soft murmurs of pleasure loosened up like stones in his throat. While they were yet children, with only a few years separating them, Julia would occasionally read aloud to him: though it was plain that he never understood what the story was about, her voice seemed to quieten him when he was restive. The children of the neighborhood always included him in their play. His joy in playing It or Hide-go-seek, especially in the summer evenings when the streetlight was on, was so poignant to Elisabeth that in spite of her trepidations—that he might fall and injure himself as he ran after the children, or that he would hide somewhere and forget his way home again, she allowed him to play. She herself sat on the front porch watching. Perhaps she had even encouraged the neighborhood children to try to share their games with Rolande, hoping it might heal or help. Julia had not understood what her sister's thoughts must have been as from her porch she sat watching Rolande, engaged in his still-innocent games.

Elisabeth lived on Bierne Street, a dead end street with an empty lot at the bend in its horseshoe curve. On summer nights the neighborhood children would play under the street lamp until nine or ten o'clock at night. Rolande too would run about under the light of the street lamp, its artificial moon irradiating the insect-laden nimbus above his head.

The night seemed to please him: sometimes he would stop short in his lurching run to gaze up at the street lamp, at the particles of dust and tiny bursts of fireflies bursting round him like blinking stars. The children would call to him that he must *run and hide, run and hide, hiding was part of the game.* They would seem to forget that he could not understand a single rule of their games. At such moments he seemed to Julia rather like some romantic poet throwing himself on the mercy of the west wind or the annealing song of the nightingale. From the distance she and Elisabeth could hear the melody of automobile horns tooting on the summer air.

But Julia noticed how her sister began to watch, at first with timid awe, then with anxiety, as Rolande's loping walk seemed suddenly to become energetic jumps, and even his shambling gait seemed but some unfocused image of a manly stride. From his sopranoed voice emerged a hoarseness, and on his impeccable skin a furor of pimples.

Then Julia noticed one summer evening something which she thought she had not observed before: that Elisabeth never once left the front porch. So long as Rolande was playing with the children, her sister stood at the porch rail, lifting her cold cup of tea now with one hand, now with the other, like some spiritual exercise or mantric prayer filled with resolve and despair. Now and then Elisabeth would read, or pretend to read, holding a newspaper or magazine in front of her face; but she did not sit down. From time to time, lowering her magazine, she would smile down at the children fleeing like a flock of birds from some imagined scarecrow, while the one who was It tried to catch them. Now and then some born prevaricator would deny he had been tagged, he would demand a second chance, appealing to Elisabeth to testify on his behalf. But Elisabeth always maintained she could not tell, she could not judge, they must not expect her to decide.

One evening by some unaccountable clutch of circumstance Rolande was It: he was to catch and tag the other children. At first the children were pleased and surprised to see that Rolande appeared to have grasped the game and that he responded with a kind of serious enthusiasm, as if he had been assigned a post of responsibility on the high seas. He began to pursue them. Screaming with delight and perhaps charmed by Rolande's impressive strength and height which seemed to promise excitement without danger, the children ran from him with glee: Rolande's hobbled gait seemed expressly designed for their teasing and evasion.

But Rolande became hot and began to perspire; the children were evading his touch all too easily; he seemed at first perplexed, then annoyed, then angry. Tears of frustration and rage ran down his face. With a rush of impatience he finally caught four-year old Lawrence Burke, holding the little fellow suspended in the air by one arm while Lawrence screamed with impotent rage, kicking his legs and looking for all the world like a flapping fowl. Elisabeth dropped her tea cup with a

"But Julia noted how her sister began to watch ...."

clattering sound and ran down the steps.

"Stop! You're too tired. *Tired! Bed. Bed. Go to bed. Go home! Go home!*" she commanded, striking Rolande's forearm with the full force of her fist, as though he were a cow or steer that had refused to budge. In a moment she would perhaps have thrown herself upon him in an effort to wrestle him to the ground. But momentarily amazed by the apparition of his mother shouting at him under the street light, he loosened his grip on little Lawrence's arm: the boy scrambled home sobbing and terrified (terrified beyond what made any sense, everyone said: Rolande had never hurt anybody in his life). And the incident was forgotten by everyone except Elisabeth.

She began waking the boy up almost at dawn, hoping perhaps to tire him out so that he would not play so fast or so hard by evening time. She even considered certain recommended sedatives, but her heart constricted at the thought: it seemed monstrous that she herself should deliberately darken the glimmerings of understanding which she had watched so slowly evolve—not light enough to survive without her help, but understanding enough at least on a summer day to find his own home from the others on the horseshoe street.

But the following year when, due to the unseasonably warm Spring the children had begun earlier than usual to celebrate their festivals of baseball and hopscotch and kickball and street lamp games, hiding exultantly in secret places, there was another incident.

The age group on their street had changed somewhat; some of the children who had been playing in the street for nearly a decade now disdained to participate. Girls who only the summer before would have hidden behind a garage or even under the summer furniture to escape being "caught" now dressed themselves self-consciously in light summer frocks and paraded themselves through the neighborhood. They walked up and down Bierne Street as if it had been a Spanish plaza. Arm in arm they rounded the street, usually pausing for particular privacy at the curving mid-point, where there was no house but only a field of dandelions and overgrown grass. There, Maryellen Contreras and Barbara Leakey and Little Bit Enders (now astonishingly grown up), would pause a while, confessing to each other in soft murmurs and an occasional bright laugh, their feuds and follies.

On this evening, as usual, the younger children were playing their games. Rolande was not It; he was merely supposed to be running away in order to be caught. But seeing how the boy who *was* It had caught a child and triumphantly tagged him with a simultaneous shove and pull, Rolande began likewise to try to tag all the children, including Maryellen, Barbara and Little Bit as the girls made their round of the street. He was especially drawn to Maryellen who wore a taffeta turquoise skirt made iridescent by the flickering evening light. Elisabeth afterwards insisted that Rolande thought the three girls were also playing the game and that believing himself to be It, he wished only to tag them. He first "caught" the two other girls, pulling them away from Maryellen, knocking them to the sidewalk by the force of his grip. Then with a strange sound in his throat as though a branch had cracked and fallen, Rolande "caught" Maryellen, pulling her turquoise skirt. Maryellen grew frightened and ran home trembling and screaming and *humiliated to the soul* (as she said) *to have had her evening walk ruined by that ape.* In her anguish, Elisabeth had struck Rolande where he stood dismayed and uncomprehending on the suddenly empty sidewalk.

It was the crisis of Elisabeth's life. She lived and relived the moment in fear and trembling: the apparently happy game under the street lamp, Rolande running cheerfully back and forth, the moment of his attraction to the iridescent skirt, and finally, his desire to "catch" the girls, followed by Maryellen's screaming and all games stopping—a film gone motionless—while the children stared at the widow Wedemeyer who had gone mad and was striking her son with furious despair.

What appeared to hurt Elisabeth most about the incident was that Rolande did not bear a grudge against her for striking him in the street, that he had felt no shame. For a while afterwards, however, he did become more quiet and tractable, so that Elisabeth began to hope that shame had split open the seed of consciousness and that he knew, he *knew* (she prayed for a sense of knowledgeable guilt) why she had struck him in fear and despair.

Several weeks later Elisabeth was sitting thus precariously balanced between anguish and hope when two men abruptly turned into their street. She was at once inexplicably relieved that Rolande was taking his nap. She had been making a shirt for Rolande and was at that moment embroidering an initial onto the pocket (she liked to decorate Rolande's shirts with such an intaglioed identity, hoping that should he get lost somewhere this silken brand of love would identify him as a creature to be tenderly treated and not one to be hauled away like a vagrant or miscreant). Carefully she set the shirt aside. She was always to remember the way the needle held straight as an arrow in the heart of the R, for at the exact moment that the men stopped at her house, she rose from her chair and the bright red thread slipped the eye of the needle; she never finished the shirt.

The men were not like any she had ever met before; their manners were painfully precise, as though sharpened for the occasion. They wore hats which they removed at once in her presence, in a sort of gentlemanly way, holding them under one arm as though shielding their heart or a revolver. Elisabeth's eye kept returning to what seemed to her these awkward but ceremonial hats, as if the secret of their intent lay hidden there.

"Mrs. Wedemeyer," said the smaller, neater one (he had introduced himself, but she had not heard his name). He seemed to Elisabeth more intelligent than the other; his dark eyes shone above a spotlessly white shirt. In spite of the heat, he seemed cool and at his ease, his face was not, like the other man's, beaded in sweat. His companion, burdened by a great superfluity of flesh, was perspiring profusely. For some reason this reminded her that Rolande had grown much heavier of late: she could not keep him from overeating—he loved, above all, to eat sugar wafers for dessert or at any time at all. He became upset if she tried to ration them. And since he rarely exercised, she worried that ....

"... so we've come from the Social Services Agency."

Elisabeth became obstinately silent. She felt at once that she and Rolande were under indictment: anything she said would be held against them.

"We've been asked to interview your son."

"*Interview?*" An abyss opened before her, created by the disparity between their expectations and her bitter knowledge. "You can't. He's sleeping."

The slim one seemed to have some sort of authority. "That's all right. Wake him up."

That he did not say *please* was what convinced Elisabeth that she was about to lose Rolande. "What do you want? He hasn't done anything ...." She knew the mere fact of her denial incriminated Rolande, but she was not able to stop the defense from tumbling from her lips: how much cleverness she needed to protect Rolande! She burst into tears.

"Not yet he hasn't—and to spare you from having to say otherwise someday, we've come here to help you."

"*Help* me! You've come to hurt my boy."

"No, we've come to save him."

"I don't need you to save him. He's mine. Nobody can save him for me." She thought she was yelling, but her voice was a hoarse cry.

"He's a threat to himself and others," said the heavy one tersely, and exchanged glances with his companion.

At this point they pulled up chairs, flanking her on either side, and began to explain to her Rolande's rights. The state could not, they said, *force* her to commit him, unless of course Rolande had committed a crime. But could she bear the responsibility for that crime, once committed? The sound of *commit, committed, commitment* roiled in her brain: *Committere*, meaning what? She could not remember what, in a schoolgirl's Latin, it had once meant.

"Have the neighbors—?" she began guardedly, wondering which of them had betrayed her.

"We do have here a complaint from the parents of Maryellen Contreras." There was a long hush, while Elisabeth refused to contradict or even acknowledge what they were saying; then the slim one said: "You can't let your son become a danger and a liability to the community!"

74

On this particular afternoon Julia had been sent to Bierne Street by her parents to bring a package to Elisabeth. It was also tacitly understood that Julia's presence there would relieve her sister for an hour or two from her perpetual vigil: Elisabeth might go out shopping or have her hair cut. As she approached her sister's front porch she saw Elisabeth entering the house, followed by the two men: they were about to waken Rolande for an interview. Silent as smoke, Julia drifted in after them: she knew enough to know that neither her sister nor the men would want her there.

Her sister was plainly nervous. She held her cupped hand to her mouth as though preparing to mime a warning to Rolande or to stifle her own outcries. She cracked the door of Rolande's room, making no sound—though waking Rolande was exactly what the men wanted her to do. From out of the narrow slit of darkness came the warm smell of urine, which Julia knew would be bitterly humiliating: her sister worked like a slave to keep Rolande clean. And she succeeded too, at least while he was awake and before the public eye: she could not wholly protect him while he slept, though she always got him up at least once during the night.

He lay dressed in his shorts. In the past year he had grown dark, curling hair in what seemed to Julia the most improbable places—on his thighs and even his heavy white chest burdened with flesh. He had been perspiring. Elisabeth laid her hand on his brow, wiping back the dampened hair. Rolande opened his eyes at her touch, looked at the men beside her, and seemed to believe he was still asleep. He smiled at them as though they were more of those strange images he saw when he slept: they came and went, changing into other forms. He appeared to go back to sleep.

Elisabeth struggled to pull him up. "Wake up, Rolande. Wake up."

"Make him stand up," said the heavy one gruffly, averting his eyes.

"*Up*, Rolande," Elisabeth commanded, as sternly as she could.

Rolande stood up. He was nearly as tall as the strangers who had come to see him. Looking only at the floor, Elisabeth led him to the bathroom: everyone pretended not to see that he had awakened just like any normal boy, his sex erect with adolescent dreams.

"What's your name?" asked one of the men of Rolande. Both men took out their notebooks.

Rolande seemed not to hear the question, or if he did, appeared to expect Elisabeth to explain everything to them, to create a benign atmosphere of tolerance or guilt as the interrogators gradually understood that but-for-the-grace-of-God their own bewildered genes would have gone the way of this ordeal. Elisabeth stood in silent despair. She could no longer conceal anything from these interviewers—chatter them no tales, offer them no explanations: to describe how her husband had deserted her after Rolande was born would not save her. Slowly, laboriously, Elisabeth began to dress him. Julia could hear her sister's heavy breathing as she half-lifted Rolande into his trousers, pulled them up around his legs, cinched his waist with a belt, knelt down to tie his shoes. Rolande smiled at them all while his mother combed his hair. The men stood in absolute silence, watching: it was as if this was what they had come to witness, this holy sacrifice, and not—as the world falsely accused them—the antics of her idiot son.

A half hour later the men, now wearing their hats, stood in Elisabeth's living room inscribing the details of Rolande's childhood, dates and numbers which Elisabeth, in a broken voice, forced one by one from her throat. Finally they left.

Their report recommended that Mr. Rolande Wedemeyer be committed to a state institution. Elisabeth was asked to appear downtown for an interview. Several persons in authority, including a psychologist and a social worker, questioned her about Rolande. They unanimously advised that "for the sake of innocent persons Mr. Wedemeyer should be placed in an institution where he would receive the proper care and where he would no longer constitute a threat either to himself or others." They wanted to emphasize that the final decision must be hers, Mrs. Wedemeyer's. But should Rolande ever commit some crime (unnamed), the burden of guilt, the *unbearable* burden of guilt, would also be hers. And so, it was Mrs. Wedemeyer herself who must decide. *Not* to decide, they concluded, was also to decide.

Several weeks passed and Elisabeth continued to declare to Julia and to their parents that no *absolute* decision was necessary (Elisabeth clung to the notion of a relative decision, a kind of hung jury which would somehow allow her and Rolande to go free ....) As Elisabeth let the months drift by, it became more evident to them all that Rolande was a grown man. Elisabeth began to dress him in more childish clothes: she also began to shave him regularly, not once but twice every day, morning and late afternoons so that there would not be the least growth visible to friends who stopped by to visit. Rolande's voice, which had begun to click-clack like a toy train, now became a bellowing bass, exploding now and then into a snort of something very like laughter.

Then one night at about two in the morning, feeling an inexplicable anguish and emptiness of soul, Elisabeth had waked with a headache. Barefooted, holding her head with pain, she had staggered to the bathroom for aspirin and water. At the sight of Rolande's open door her heart had seemed to stop: he was not in his bed. The front door was flung open as if he had fled in great haste or been kidnapped. The drilling headache not-forgotten but accepted now, as if it too were all a part of her expiation for some forgotten sin, she rushed to the front porch.

It was a cloudy night with no moon. Only the street lamp beamed the desolate street, its light honed to a single inquisitorial spot. A few cats were roaming the dark: Elisabeth nearly fainted when one of them rushed at her legs. Trembling, she apostrophized the night, making a pact with the power that controlled her fate: *Let him come, let him appear. Only let him be safe. Let him not have hurt ... himself, and I'll give him up. For his own sake, I'll give him up.*

She was whimpering aloud. Had policemen driven onto their street at that moment and spotted her in her bare feet and nightdress, her hair wildly disheveled, they would perhaps have taken her into custody.

But there was no one. Instinctively she first ran the entire length of the street: but without calling Rolande. Above all, she did not want to waken her neighbors. She ran, peering into the front porches and backyards: the sight of clothes left overnight on their lines, flapping like beckoning arms, terrified her. A dog began to bark at her; she returned to the street. It was still deserted. She forced herself to the empty field: it was astonishing how she ran to it, in spite of her terror. She thanked God there were probably no snakes in the city. But there were plenty of stones and bushes; their thorns tore at her nightdress. She thought she saw a rat .... She recoiled in horror, but she had not the strength at that moment to return home for her shoes, she had only sufficient strength to go on. Then she heard a sound, which she prayed was Rolande, but she was not certain. It was soft and vibrant, it seemed to her not deep enough to be Rolande's voice. She stood motionless, unable to go farther. If not Rolande, who was it? Again came a sort of murmuring undertone. Suppose she simply uncovered a pair of Bierne Street lovers lying in the grass? But that was an idle hope, meant to distract her from her fear. She stood listening to the murmuring sounds. They grew now softer, now louder. With a quaking heart, she felt it must be Rolande, and yet it could not be he: she had never heard these intonations, this incantation of sorrow and grief, like a man made mad by joy and longing. If she had brought a flashlight .... Her heart leaped with relief at a sound which she distinctly recognized to be Rolande, but sank with dread at the realization that he was "talking" to someone who did not reply. Trembling so that she could barely stand, she approached the voice with anguish, with remorse, though never—not even long after-wards—did she admit to herself the true source of her terror. She found Rolande lying in the tall grass, Maryellen's turquoise skirt in his arms. In dread, her eyes scoured the surrounding grass: nothing—only the turquoise skirt. Rolande lay in the grass embracing the skirt, holding it to his lips, caressing it. Almost for the first time she was struck by the size of his hands: he could have held a kicking sheep in his hands and it would not have escaped him. At first Rolande did not even see her; he was intent on his litany. He continued to speak to the lightly billowing skirt, murmuring in the soft humming monotone which Elisabeth had mistaken for another voice; he sobbed, he caressed the cloth, he wiped his eyes with it, he sniffed as if its fragrance were a flower: he had learned grief overnight, and though he knew not what tormented him, he was suffering all the agonies of love.

"Rolande!" she called in a sharp whisper. Then more gently, her heart softening at the sight of his suffering, "Rolande ...." He raised his face. Her eyes filled with tears: *the dear child knows his name.*

He raised his face from the folds of the skirt. Tears coursed down his cheeks, but his face was radiant: she had never seen him so happy.

"Go home, Rolande," she commanded sorrowfully.

To her surprise he dug in his heels in stubborn refusal; it was the first time he had ever refused to obey her outright command. "Go home, I say!" she repeated with sorrow and fury.

Rolande threw himself flat on the ground, covering the skirt. Elisabeth began to struggle with him for possession of the cloth, now soiled with stains. It smelled faintly of dried asters or chrysanthemums. Rolande would not release it. She would have to use it both as a leash and a lure: she allowed him to keep one end of it while she held the other. In this way, with Rolande lurching behind her, they made their way from the field, carrying Maryellen's raiment between them like a litter. At one point Elisabeth stumbled over a stone and fell; but neither she nor Rolande would relax their hold on the skirt, and it tore in their hands.

For the first time in her life Elisabeth gave him drugs to make him sleep. Her hand trembled as she counted the drops, red as cordial, into his milkcup. Holding his head up like a sick patient while he continued to clutch the torn skirt, she fed it to him in small sips. She waited with a thudding heart, like a plotting murderer, till he had fallen asleep. Then she put on her shoes, and remembering this time to take a flashlight with her, she returned to the field to seek what with all her heart she prayed not to find.

Every step she took was a prayer, every sudden sound evoked from her a vow: *Let it not have happened and I'll give him up. Let ....* Over and over she crossed the empty field with her flashlight. Every scrap of paper, every broken branch with its torn leaves stopped her heart. The scream of a cat made her cry out in fright, it was so human. But she persevered, she forced herself onward; she looked, even, under a big rock, her eyes glued with horror to the sight of the scurrying ants and pillbugs and centipedes who flowed into the beam of her light. But she did not wholly trust the limited beam of her flashlight, she decided to wait for daybreak and then continue her search. She returned to the front porch, hiding behind the chairs for fear her neighbors would notice her. At last the first signs of daybreak lightened the sky. Lurching with exhaustion, she forced herself back to the field to look leaf by leaf and stone by stone for what she at last believed, sobbing with relief, she would not find.

Her neighbors found her asleep on the steps of her house, the flashlight still in her hand: she had crossed and recrossed the empty lot for five hours, relentlessly pursuing the girl whose mute body would have called her son a madman.

A week later, when the men from the social agency returned for a second interview, Elisabeth and Rolande climbed into their small car: Rolande, a big smiling boy who might have been on a family outing, sat alone in the back seat looking out the window at his neighbors. By four o'clock in the afternoon, in accordance with Elisabeth's signed consent, Rolande was committed to an Institute for Exceptional Children: she had saved him from love.

HEROES

"… the heroic in human affairs.
Too evidently this is a large topic;
deserving quite other treatment than
we can expect to give it at present."

Thomas Carlyle

When she was young and lived in a college town not far from home, Karen believed in Truth, Love, Fame, and Immortal Fame. The most important ideas at that time were certain to come in capital letters, including Death. When a professor wrote in the margin of a paper she'd done on *Aucassin and Nicolette*, "Why is Beauty capitalized?" she'd at first planned an impressive reply, then, feeling threatened by the question which seemed at once stupid and penetrating, she'd explained to herself that the professor was a mere Academic: Truth was Beauty and Beauty Truth, and both were going to be a joy to her forever. She proceeded, therefore, to broaden her philosophical system into other Capitals: Courage, Youth, Passion, and Lust-for-Life.

Above all, Art. It was for Art's sake, obviously, that Milton had been condemned to blindness, Beethoven to deafness, Pope to monstrosity, Toulouse-Lautrec to dwarfism, and Gauguin to elephantiasis: Suffering begat the Sublime and the Beautiful, she'd learned that lesson early, not from Longinus, but from Daniel Lantho, the day they'd all been on a field trip to the Museum. Miss Halprin had been leading her senior class, enjoying her students' freedom as much as her own. Suddenly, tall reedy Daniel Lantho had stumbled at the eroded curbstone and fallen into the street. He lay there groaning, his ankle sprained. Promptly Miss Halprin called out: "Suffering is good for the soul, Daniel," and with warmth—in fact, with Zest—urged Daniel to walk on it, to bear up under it, and above all, to observe the paintings he was about to see, as it were, through his cloud of pain. "You just wait, Daniel," Miss Halprin promised. "You'll do a better drawing for this experience, you'll see."

They'd all laughed at this—at Daniel sprawled and groaning, at Miss Halprin, pedagogic and zestful—but they'd believed her too, and paid special attention to Daniel's drawing at the next meeting of the art class. Sure enough, Daniel's drawing had been better than any of the others. Compared to him, they had all—including Karen—done numb representations in crude watercolor or drawn straight lines with a ruler meant to represent the Greek columns holding the Museum erect. Karen later asked Daniel whether he thought the pain of his ankle had contributed anything to his drawing. "Well," he said slowly, "it did make me think." Karen staggered away, reeling from the intensity of Daniel's eyes, a blue as bright as turquoise set in a ring of bone. That night she worked on an acrostic until two a.m., rather regretting that *Daniel* had so few letters, she'd have preferred a Spenserian stanza. But she was content, the Experience had enriched her life: Love and Youth became fused with Art, a holy trinity of which Daniel had taken on the human form.

She began looking for Daniel where she could, lingering near his locker, or strolling across the football field, her textbooks plausibly crushed to her bosom. It was the season of the Decathlon Meets, and she soon observed that Daniel's preference was for pole vaulting. No doubt Daniel hoped to be famous for pole vaulting just as she meant to make a name for herself writing interpretations of George Eliot, George Meredith and George Sand. Three afternoons a week, cunningly disguised in sunglasses, a workingman's kerchief and worn jeans, she sat in the bleachers watching the athletes. Daniel's performance was flawless. With a single luminous leap he catapulted through space; then, like a mountain skier, he descended invisible slopes of air till he landed upright and unharmed.

Inspired by the vision, Karen composed an allegory in which Daniel was suitably personified as Prometheus; the poem delighted her, but her sense of appropriateness wavered when one afternoon Daniel's leap trembled, the invisible valley of air beneath him crumbled, and Daniel fell in a heap to the ground.

For weeks Daniel lay in the hospital, his leg in a plaster cast. Karen, along with three or four others from Halprin's Class, came to the hospital to visit, listening to Daniel describe the logistics of doing his trigonometry in bed and of learning to look into a microscope from a horizontal position. Soon, he promised, he would be able to do everything upside down, like a fly. Karen noticed that his voice cracked slightly as he joked, perhaps from the hilarity of his imagination or from the strain of being surrounded by Youth, Beauty, and All-His-Admirers.

Daniel celebrated his eighteenth birthday in the hospital, so he graduated a year later than everybody else in Halprin's Class. Karen lost touch with him for a while. When he eventually joined the others at the State University, most of those who had been in their class had become sophisticated sophomores, pledged to fraternity houses and sororities; some were already getting married; some were taking their Sophomore Year Abroad.

The first time Karen passed Daniel on the Quad, he appeared not to know her: of course, she'd never really been His Girl, only an admirer, he'd never known that for her he'd been the embodiment of Love, Youth, Art, Fame and Courage: so she freely forgave him for not recognizing her. Karen hesitated a moment, then came closer, smiling at him in dramatic recognition, noticing at once how his eyes were now a

"His dark hair was seeded with grey, his eyes were narrow and angry ...."

Mediterranean blue, changing in color according to the light. He stared at her in surprise, but when she reminded him that he was the famous pole vaulter who had broken his leg in his senior year, an ecstatic smile illumined his face. Then, almost at once, his face became nonchalant: he had never pole vaulted again, he said.

Karen waited expectantly for his epic tale—of days of immobilization, of nights of agony, of the dramatic moment when the doctor would have told him he might never walk again (she glanced down at his leg, ready to discern a barely discernible limp), and was dismayed to hear that his reason for giving it up had been something less than metaphorical: he'd been afraid of another accident. "Another broken leg, and I'd not have been able to take my summer job." He explained that he worked every summer for Parks and Recreation—it earned him enough for tuition, he added, his face becoming even more nonchalant.

But Karen scarcely heard him, she felt disillusioned, it wasn't the story she'd meant to hear. It was, rather, like passing the kitchen of an elegant restaurant where, instead of the delectable dishes with names like humming birds (*pâté de foie gras, volailles à blanc, escargots*), one saw the snails lying in the barrel or the goose hanging by its feet. The moment in which she'd intended to express admiration for his Struggle now yielded only embarrassment. With sudden abruptness Daniel excused himself and left her standing alone on the Quad. For a long time afterwards she was troubled by this meeting, trying to understand what it had really meant. Finally she opted for Disillusion (hers), in spite of which she crafted an excellent *Ubi sunt*—avoiding any reference to the Sublime, and afterwards put the poem away in a drawer and Daniel out of her mind: she was within a hexameter of calling her former hero a Coward.

But it was one thing to inter Daniel as a symbol of her (own) Youthful Idealism, and quite another to forget him altogether. For one thing, she kept meeting him on the Quad. Every morning that winter she had an eight o'clock class, and as she crossed over from the arboretum on the way to Fine Arts, she'd reach the Quad intersection at the same time Daniel did. The wind was biting at that hour of the morning, before the sun had first melted, then glazed the snow-covered grass, and Daniel would be walking hunched over in his wind breaker, his hands in his pockets, his dark hair covered with snow. Sometimes he wore an army surplus jacket; on those mornings he looked grimmer than ever, his eyes cold metal clips. He'd pivot somewhat against the wind as they passed, bending his shoulder as if the biting air had just struck him an especially telling blow. "Hi Karen," he'd say tonelessly.

Daniel's mood was contagious, and that semester Karen did more brooding than studying; she failed algebra and became ill in biology lab on Tuesday and Thursday afternoons, sickened by the foetal-looking frogs and the terrifying reality of their intestines. Fortunately, afterwards she was able to sit around at The Pretzel Jar, drinking cokes with her friends while they gave her advice, lecturing her in a gentle way about her habit of wearing tartan skirts with checkered blouses. Sometimes they would gossip about Daniel Lantho. There were two rumors afloat about him—one that he'd slipped across the border to avoid the draft, the other that he'd been sent to jail for the possession of drugs. Neither of these turned out to be true: rather, Daniel had got married to a girl named Lisa whom he'd met while visiting some distant relatives in New Orleans, and then he'd been promptly shipped out to Vietnam.

At first Karen and her friends made an effort to get to know Lisa, but their attempts were thwarted by what they thought of as Lisa's difficult personality. One day, for instance, when Karen was at Shoppers' Mall picking up an electric cooker (she was into crockery cooking) she approached Lisa who'd been standing at a nearby counter buying an alarm clock. She and Lisa exchanged a few words, Lisa replying in an oddly throaty voice, as though choked with several emotions at once. Karen noticed that her eyes were plum-colored and rather protuberant, which made her seem either unnaturally clever or unusually stupid. When Karen invited her to lunch, she'd stood still several moments in silence, looking rather like one of those small animals trapped in one's headlights, then she'd murmured an excuse and fled. Karen was distinctly disappointed, and reported back to her friends that Lisa was "quite inarticulate." After one or two similar experiences they all agreed that Lisa was Nothing, nothing at all.

So when Daniel left for Vietnam, those who'd known him in Halprin's Class, and who said they were very sympathetic to the situation, felt themselves to be in rather an awkward spot. They didn't really know Lisa very well, they said, and now it was too late to cultivate her. Then they got news that Lisa was pregnant, and that she'd taken a job in the city. Commuting back and forth took up all Lisa's time, her private concerns made her life marginal to theirs, rendering her, so to speak, *hors de combat*: they were all relieved not to have to make a personal decision about it.

Those were tumultuous, destructive times; a few young men Karen had known in Halprin's Class had become war resisters, some were into dope and had dropped out of sight into a culture of their own, still others had already returned from Vietnam, and now sat around with disheveled hair, wearing their worn jeans like combat fatigues. Two young men whom Karen had dated left for Vietnam: one returned after a year, went into business and never spoke of it again; the other remained in a Veterans' Hospital. For those who, like Karen, had remained at home, time passed, not in a continuum, but in the eruption of events, like the mass arrests in Washington or the invasion of Cambodia; after which, for a while, silence would reign. Counting up all her time, Karen discovered that while the war had been going on, she'd accumulated enough credits to be able to graduate during the summer if she would take courses instead of taking a vacation in Mexico.

She chose to study, and thus was on campus when Lisa had her baby. Daniel was still in Saigon at the time. Lisa now no longer commuted to the city but sat on the front porch reading while the baby slept in a wicker basket beside her. Karen, on her way to sociology class, would see Lisa sometimes, writing letters on pale blue overseas stationery, or holding the baby to her bosom. The sight of Mother and Child together on the front porch filled Karen with longing. For several weeks she dreamed of exquisite layettes and smooth arms held protectively around an infant in blue bunting. She even thought for a while that to have one of these babes in arms she ought perhaps to marry Si Burns, who was the son of a local druggist and rode a Yamaha. But it was her year for Study Abroad, so Karen was parcelled off to Avignon where she learned a great deal of French and when she returned, Si was married to someone else. The house where Lisa had lived was now occupied by an old woman with an attack dog chained to a peeling white column on the porch. The dog's fierce barking filled Karen with something like guilt, as if she were in fact an intruder. She meant to knock on the door of the house and inquire of the new occupant what had happened to Lisa and the baby, their whereabouts, etc. But the dog blocked her approach to the house; and in fact until the day of her graduation, she would cross over to the far side of the street rather than pass in front of the dog. After several months the dog had seemed to know Karen and stopped barking at her, but she continued to cross over to the other side out of habit. She was at that time quite preoccupied with taking the Graduate Record Examination and the Advanced Placement Examination, and in making up a small loss she'd suffered somewhere in Medieval French, so when she ran across Daniel again outside one of the buildings, she was shocked. His dark hair was seeded with grey, his eyes were narrow and angry, there was a faint tremor in his hands. She tried to remember what was the appropriate thing to say to someone you'd loved who stood before you, an early-aging man with trembling hands, his voice fleeing for cover like an animal that hears fire in the ground.

"How are you?" she asked at last.

He nodded, as if in agreement with something, but did not answer. "You know about Lisa," he said presently. She didn't; she felt guilty, she should have crossed over to the porch to inquire, but since she hadn't, she remained silent, forgetting even to show sympathy or shock as he explained to her that the baby had never really been 'right.' "Its head was always, you know, sort of too big ...." Daniel pulled savagely at his eyebrows, as if wrenching the words from his skull. "She should have gone down home to her mother's," he said, "instead of riding it out alone. As for me ... I wasn't in any shape to help her, how could I of been?"

She dared not ask where Lisa was now, she felt he had left most of it unexplained, he wouldn't talk about it here. Perhaps he would tell her if they were alone. The cashier had now rung up all his purchases, he could wait for her outside if he wished. Karen wanted to say "Wait for me," but the fact that he was a married man alone rooted her tongue: wouldn't she be Misunderstood?

After her groceries were bagged, she hurried out, she looked up and down the street, hoping he'd lingered. But the sunlit street was empty.

The next she heard of him was at a June wedding: she was clutching the bridal bouquet she had just caught when someone whispered, "Do you know Daniel's in the VA hospital?"

Daniel was put on methadone for about a year, and when he got out of the VA hospital, Karen had already been married for several months to a pleasant chemist from England: she adored his accent and was pleased to hear people say she was lucky not to have to compete since he was a Scientist and she was "in" Literature. Indeed, she was glad Morris didn't compete, though she sometimes felt it would have been nice to have shared an aubade or two. Still, if they didn't exactly understand each other, at least (as they frequently said) they didn't quarrel about anything either. They were in agreement too that they should wait to have children until Morris had finished his graduate work and had a secure position in the private sector rather than in the university where, they agreed, scientists were dreadfully underpaid.

Karen had begun to feel she had travelled far indeed from the girl who had sat in the bleachers watching the pole vaulters: so it was a real shock to her when, while crossing the street, a shiny yellow hat bobbed up from a trench in the earth one day, rather like a metallic sunflower sprung from the ruins, and Daniel called out, "Hi there, Karen. Still hitting the books?" Daniel's back was stripped bare to the blazing sun, the sweat ran down his forehead in two small fissures, glinting in the light like steel. Stunned at the apparition, Karen raised a handkerchief to her lips as if to pat the perspiration away, but she was not perspiring at all, rather she felt utterly cold with something like fear. Daniel leaped from the pit where he and a work crew had been laying a gas main. Unabashed at his nakedness and his sweat, he came up very close to her because of the street noises, shook her hand vigorously, and yelled in her ear. "Had a baby yet?" She shook her head. "Got a husband, *that* I see," glancing at her ring. She nodded again. He lifted his head as if to look at the sun from a new angle. I'm back in school myself. Kicked the habit clean, you know? You heard about Lisa, I guess? After two years, they said she was perfectly well, they let her go home. And she'd hardly been home for a month when she ran away again. Like she was really into the drug scene. She never did get over Petit-chou's not being like other kids. Like it was something we'd done to him .... O'D'd in San Francisco, at least that's what they told me, you have to take them at their word: I couldn't prove anything one way or the other ...."

Karen realized with a jolt that she didn't know the baby's name, his real name: it was a secret Daniel had shared with Lisa, and which she was now not likely ever to share.

"Well, I guess I better get back to work. A couple more hours and I'll be heading over to the Quad. Ever see any of Halprin's gang?"

Karen meant to reply in a light-hearted joking way that yes, she still saw them occasionally, that they were all well, at least as well as could be expected, considering who they were. But she hesitated, her voice choking with emotion.

"Yes," she said at last. "I see them from time to time. They're ... all grown up now."

Daniel stared at her a long while, as if trying to decide whether she meant by that anything he wanted to understand. The sun blazed down. He picked up his shovel; the turquoise eyes shone through the sweat, a silver setting around the Indian blue.

"It's about time," he said, tilting his hat at the sun.

PILLARS OF LOVE

S napping his lunch box shut was like setting off the Westclox: Julia came into the kitchen, set the baby in the high chair, gave Reffie an awkward hug. Noticing Reffie's still-open jacket, she buttoned it for him, straight to the throat: he understood that this was purely talismanic, meant to ward off pneumonia and other bad things from the mine; so he stood patient as a horse, grateful for the attention, knowing he would unbutton his jacket the moment he was out of sight.

Behind him now the click of the door locking itself into place— though not against burglars and thieves. The other miners swore that there had not been a burglary in the Valley as far back as they could rightly remember: you could leave your car unlocked too, they added, to really impress Reffie. In a town like this, where everybody knows everybody else, nobody would steal anything from you, they said: you couldn't lose anything if you tried, they'd be sure to find it for you and give it back to you.

Except your life, his friend Smetka had retorted, smiling.

But on such a beautiful day Reffie was not going to think Morbid Thoughts. The miners all joked—at once facetiously and seriously— that thinking Morbid Thoughts caused vibrations in the ceilings; the more you dwelt on such things the more likely the earth would tremble and mysterious canyons open up before you. Heading toward Main Street Reffie turned right. There was never much traffic off the steep road from his house; he preferred to approach the mine by way of the town rather than by crossing the hillside horizontally to descend by way of an overgrown path. That way he was more likely to see a few folks before punching his clock, store up some faces before going under-ground. And he liked looking into the store windows, too, seeing the shops open up as he headed toward the mine gate. He'd got into a superstitious habit of forecasting his luck for the day by the kind of company he saw on the way to work: the postman, the grocer, the lady from Ladies Apparel, and especially the school kids. He loved to see them heading for school, their eyes still glazed with sleep, a quiet pride in their walk: the great thing about the kids here, they seemed so free and unafraid, as if they believed that no matter what happened in the rest of the country, they could always survive somehow, living in a hut in the wilderness, maybe, trapping small game and fish from the lake.

Now at the corner of South Bitteroot and Main, Reffie paused. This was Grampa Wing's favorite view of the town. Grampa had watched the streets of the Valley and the deep levels of the mine grow together: his first job had been in the mine. Grampa had seen how the town grew, first attracting a small seed and grain supply house and a grain elevator along the railroad spur; then had come what Grampa still called a saloon, then a barber shop followed by the still-operating Buckholtz dry goods store, featuring (in Grampa's day) the best calico and muslin; and then an elite new specialization for the time—a milliner's shop, now known, though still partial to millinery, as Ladies Apparel. After that had come a second grocery, and a third and a fourth, and one that sold fresh vegetables brought to the town even in *winter*, whereas when he, Grampa Wing had been growing up, you might have had nothing but canned green beans and peas or maybe a chunk of hubbard squash. Main Street proclaimed to him the changes since those days: the town now had more than its share of doctors (one a D.O.), some of them runaways from the California freeways—self-exiled to backpacking in the wilderness; several dentists; at least a half-dozen beauty parlors (probably more, but Reffie hadn't really counted those). Exactly where it used to be, across from Ladies Apparel, was the very barber shop which Grampa claimed had been there over fifty years. It still sported its candy-striped spiral totem which still revolved ceaselessly in perfect silence, like some exotic fish undulating in a glass aquarium. Reffie had been in the barber shop for a shave and haircut one Saturday morning when his daughter Tamsen seemed about to enjoy some social life in the Valley at last—their friendly neighbor from across the street had drifted into the house unannounced—Reffie had got himself out of the house as fast as possible. On that morning, he'd sat like a Pope or a King observing Arimeo the barber with curiosity to see if he'd show some distaste at the sight of Reffie's stubbled face, which for all Reffie knew might still have a just-visible film of ore dust limning the eyelids. Reffie had stared past Arimeo's handsome young face (a Shoshone Indian, he kept his hair trimmed and glossy as an Italian prince), while Arimeo lathered up the soap and laid it on Reffie's bone-stressed cheeks, the skin fretted with hatchings that had become concave stars (they were the devil to shave). Arimeo, unlike the calumnious reports of barbers on any other Main Street, had refused to engage in conversational banter or gossip or even the state of his health: so Reffie had been reduced to contemplating his own face in the mirror. This however had brought small comfort for his human condition. Rather, the congealed Self and the silence had served somehow to spell out how close to Eternity one always was: his own facial immobility and stark staring eyes seemed even to himself already sepulchral. What he had become sadly aware of as he sat in the barber's chair—though he believed his sadness was not merely, or at least not solely, a matter of vanity—was that what had been scattered streaks of gray in his dark hair, like an uptapped vein of ore, had within the past year become a helmet of firm and timeless metal: permanent, inescapable, uniform. Looking into Arimeo's mirror he recorded this fact

"He avoided looking at Smetka's slot."

without sentiment or pity, as he would have noted that a dog or horse lies down in the dust when his time came upon him to lie down forever. Still, the eyes astonished him: he might have hoped that in some way his gaze would reflect a little of the hope and pride and even tenderness of his life; reflect perhaps the tone in which he tried, he thought, to speak to his children or even what he *didn't* say—his unspoken murmuring incantation of ache and anguish for their survival in a world fraught with danger and worry. His eyes ought to have shown that.

In alarm Reffie had turned away from the mirror: his own face had made him afraid, though he would not have admitted this to anyone. Turning for relief from this doppelgänger, Reffie had focused his sight directly out the barber shop window across Main Street into the window of Ladies Apparel, where bronze or coppery heads with silver eyes, looking as if they'd fallen from a guillotine on some red planet, were gazing at his own still-intact head. From out of their metallic stare they seemed to Reffie to have been weighing his case all along; to have been watching as first his cheeks were lathered, then restored to a near-normal condition. As Reffie sat returning the stare of these ultra-human heads (his own all-too-human head being meanwhile scraped of debris, as though he were a miner in an accident and Arimeo had been sent to rescue him) suddenly pale hands with glosswhite nails had fluttered around these bodiless Nefertitis. Their silver eyes remained unchanged, but the heads were now quickly transformed. One copper-colored head soon sported a cockaded hat; and the head which only moments before had seemed to bear the tragic mien of the guillotine became transformed by this bit-of-business into a face of mere foolishness. Even the smile seemed to dilate—charged now, it seemed to Reffie, with the cynical allure of a Lady of the Night. On a second head the agile fingers now placed a velvet fedora with feathers, not of course real feathers, like the ostrich or egret of Grampa's day, but imitation feathers resembling the equipage of a whooping crane.

But now he was no longer enjoying the show: instead he had begun to think about money, about how much hardrock one would have had to excavate in order to pay for an outfit like that. But this sort of calculation caused his pulse to quicken with anxiety; he would find himself breathing heavily, as though there had been a change in the ventilation system of the mine: a man could feel the pressure of it at once. And after he had paid Arimeo he had decided that barber shops were a luxury he could do without—he'd let Julia cut his hair, at least till he was sure the mine would stay open and if it stayed open, that they'd keep him.

At the curb of South Bitteroot he tamped down his pipe. The sun had now triumphed over the few skimming clouds: the Valley was unveiled. The sky exploded with light. Turning his head to shield his eyes from its brillance, Reffie caught an angled glimpse of a stand of firs on the hillsides, their long boles serene as cloistered monks. But now his time was up: he must walk quickly and without further pause straight to the main gate of C & L where he would punch his clock: it would be ten minutes to eight.

It was still a matter of some surprise to Reffie to see his name recorded in such clear, legible symbols, as though his name and the time of his existence were information of great import to the world at large, not meant to be lost. And a strange ritual it was, in which he was hailed daily with this subtle, Delphic message: Ambrose Raphael Wingfield. Nobody had ever called him Ambrose, and only the nurse in the Salinas hospital knew how the name of the archangel guarding our first Garden had been spelled out as Reffie.

This name now leaped to sight and alongside it, the date: with a kind of aggrieved diffidence, as if he were somehow ashamed of this indelible record of the hours of life about to be contracted to the C & L Silver-Lead & Zinc Company, Reffie punched the hour. The time clock chimed back at him, inveterately cheerful.

He avoided looking at Smetka's slot. He'd become accustomed to working with Smetka and he felt lonely without him: he'd not become friends with any other miner. Smetka was a serious hardworking young man with the troubled look of a much older man. You trusted him: when you turned toward him, you'd know he'd been watching you; but if you tried to acknowledge this in some way, with a word of gratitude or camaraderie, Smetka would shy away from it. It was Smetka who'd first taught him how to work in the hardrock. When Reffie and Julia and the kids had arrived after the long drive from Seattle, with fourteen dollars in his pocket, Reffie had parked the old Ford in front of what was to be their rented row house for the season and headed for Silver Valley to talk to the boss. Before the week was out Reffie was underground working.

Almost from his first day in the mine he and Smetka had worked well together. Smetka was quiet and brooding, with a shy smile which came and went around his mouth, while Reffie thought of himself as vocal and angry. He could not forget that his father and Gramp had been embattled union men in their day, and when he went into the underground city of silver and zinc and lead he could not remain silent. Smetka, on the other hand, who had worked in the mine for years, had learned patience: his temper remained unruffled in spite of Reffie's obvious lack of experience; he was willing to share with Reffie his hard-won knowledge. He showed Reffie his own heavy waterproof boots and told him where he might buy a pair "pretty reasonable," warned him against wandering away by himself to adjoining tunnels, offered to let Reffie watch him until Reffie had learned for himself how to stope and pillar the walls, how to handle the drill. The very first day he'd taken time out from his own work to show Reffie how to timber a ceiling, using the great logs from the nearby stands of fir. Smetka pointed out with quiet pride that the logs had been treated with the best fire-resistant oil preservative on the market, a technique Smetka himself had persuaded the company to use, and was now used all the time. Above all, Smetka had taught him how to drill a hole for explosives; how to set the dynamite and handle misfires: to learn to detonate a misfire, Smetka swore, was the sacred secret of survival.

But there were still some things—Reffie grimly admitted—that Smetka had been unable to teach him, and that was how to breathe in temperatures of a hundred and ten degrees, how to keep his eyes clear of the sweat which ran down his brow. And how to become resigned to his work: he went underground every day hoping the next day would be better, that he would become used to it, that something would happen to the economy so that he could buy some sheep or work the land again, so that Julia would not altogether run out of the hope that their marriage would bring her what he had promised.

He and Smetka were part of a six-man crew who usually worked together at an excavation, each man's skill supplementing that of the others. But since Reffie and Smetka worked so well as a team, the other men in their crew would often work another area of the tunnel, returning now and again to let them know when the explosive had been set and the area was to be evacuated. They would then have to stay out of the area for at least thirty minutes, until the fumes had diffused. At such times he and Smetka would switch to another part of the tunnel, either loading ore into the skip hoist for the smelter or sometimes just working together at the mindless job of shovelling waste rock used to stabilize the walls in stoping and pillaring. While stoping a new wall face they were careful to leave the arched pillars created by the excavation work: the arched pillars helped support the tunnel walls, prevented rockbursts. Working together, he and Smetka had never had a rockburst: this was, Reffie believed, because Smetka was the soul of caution. A modest man, Smetka merely said of himself that he might not be an engineer, but he knew a shaky pillar when he saw one.

But on this particular day, in spite of Smetka's usual precautions, due perhaps to the tremendous heat generated by the drilling of a new vein above them, there had been a rockburst: the pillars had caved in, and although neither Reffie nor Smetka had been hurt, their access to the first entry shaft was totally blocked by fallen rock. In spite of the dim light, Reffie could see, like an evolutionary trail of trilobites, the faint blue veins laminating the volcanic stone.

Smetka had remained calm. On the other side of the crumbled pillar were the rest of the crew. Reffie could still hear their voices, at least he thought they were voices: the roar of the rockburst had left a ringing in his ears. In spite of his faith in Smetka, Reffie's heart was pounding with fear. He assured himself that Smetka knew every raise and winze of the mine; he had spent most of his adult life here in this subterranean city. But as he and Smetka stood aside waiting for the final convulsion of dust and rubble, Reffie began to understand that the crumbled pillar had not only cut off access to the entry shaft but had shut off air from the surface fans ventilating the tunnels through the two shafts. Now one of their funnels of air had been tamped shut.

Smetka was not one to panic. He knew his way to the other shaft. Also, he reminded Reffie, the miners on the other side of the crumbled pillar still had access to the first entry shaft: they would alert the rescue team; the elevator cage would be waiting for Smetka and Reffie when they reached the other shaft.

"But we have to *get* to it," said Smetka. "And fast."

Their flashlights were in perfect condition, so they were able to see well enough at first; they flooded the steam-wet walls with light as they headed for a drift which Smetka said would lead them to the second shaft. "The thing is to keep calm. Try to breathe shallow."

Reffie tried to *breathe shallow*. Their flashlights played along the walls. They were now wading through muddy water, but he was not surprised. Though Reffie's own tunnels were usually dry underfoot, he'd seen the miners working with hoses, the water vapor saturating their raincoats and billed caps, the temperatures climbing to a hundred and twenty ....

They approached a drift which led to an exit tunnel. At the end of the tunnel was a ladder, which would bring them to the next level. From there, Smetka said, the cage elevator would be waiting for them, the emergency alarm would have been sounded, rescue teams would be ready at the surface. They would lift the cage elevator at double the maximum speed: risky but necessary. As they stooped to enter the rarely used drift—only the stoped-out pillars were left behind for support—a piping sound, like a pair of whistles, stopped them. Smetka played his flashlight toward the ground. Several terrified mice were plunging headlong down a slight incline. They seemed at first to be merely awkwardly slipping in the clayey deposits; but then one of them gave a desperate leap into the air, shuddered with convulsions and died.

"Suffocated. Carbon monoxide ... We can't go by way of that drift," Smetka said grimly. Quickly he made a U-turn. *He knows the mine*, his body assured Reffie. They climbed up another ladder, ran as fast as they dared across a drift. The heat seemed to melt their flesh; the sweat ran down their bodies like rain. Smetka threw off his waterproof, then his shirt, leaving his chest bare. In the midst of his deadly fear Reffie noted how thin Smetka's chest was—*nothing but skin and bone*—yet he'd seen Smetka work with a drill that must have been a third of his own weight. That he should be noticing such a thing, a fact quite irrelevant to their survival, was somehow frightening: their most urgent need was to remain rational, yet these useless thoughts flew about like chicken feathers. As they crawled through an abandoned excavation, the walls seemed to darken. Reffie could feel the sweat on him, not of heat but of fear. It was a hell of a way to die, thought Reffie, and a homesick longing for his Texas landscape hit him in the midst of a sudden fit of coughing. Then he saw that Smetka had tied a handkerchief across his mouth. Reffie did the same; but it only seemed to make things worse: it trapped the sweat rolling down his face.

But worse than the heat was the strange silence. They were accustomed to drills vibrating, periodic explosions of dynamite. But now there was nothing not a sound. If there was a rescue party set in motion, if there were sirens above ground screeching to a stop, if there were medics anxiously waiting with ambulances and oxygen, they could hear none of it. He began to fear that the men on the other side of the caved-in pillar had not, after all, been able to walk away from the rockburst to report that Reffie and Smetka were cut off. Perhaps they too at this moment were asphyxiating. Smetka was choking for breath; Reffie tried to keep his own breathing shallow and regular. But they had to move fast, nearly running, and he was forced to open his mouth to pant. The possibility of carbon monoxide in the air made it unsafe to slow down. Yet abruptly Smetka stopped, he seemed confused.

The possibility that Smetka could get lost had astonishingly not occurred to Reffie: confused, but not lost. He waited to hear Smetka assure him that it was impossible to be lost, but Smetka could not speak, he was vomiting.

"Keep going. I'll come later." Smetka leaned against the face of the hanging wall. He pointed toward a fresh vertical cut in the wall face. "They must be working that new vein they found up above us. Push yourself through there ... then along about twenty feet to your right ought to be another ladder. That'll take you to a loading station. You can come get me ...."

Reffie did not waste breath arguing. He managed to push Smetka ahead of him through the fresh cut in the hanging wall. Then with tears of relief he saw that Smetka did indeed know his mine: a new vein was being opened a few yards from the ladder. But the ladder now rose above them, nearly a hundred feet. Looking up, the parallel lines with crossing iron rungs seemed to take on a life of their own, to shift threateningly before his eyes: a grim, ominous leaning tower. Reffie removed his belt from his waist and looped it through Smetka's belt. Smetka opened his eyes momentarily, managed to support himself to the first rung of the ladder. Reffie moved ahead of him, up the ladder, gripping the belt, his hands wet with sweat. Slowly, rung by rung, using his own body as a winch around which he held the belt fast to himself he helped Smetka upward, a human bucket hoisted like ore in a skip hoist from out of that eternal dark. When, at the top of the ladder Reffie's head reached the loading level, he felt a strong surge of air coming in from the second shaft: blessed air, more vital than an ocean breeze, surged through the tunnel.

Smetka was still breathing when he laid him in the railcar. The car made its way down the tracks, maintaining a maddeningly steady pace as if it were carrying a load of waste rock. Reffie tried cooling Smetka down with his shirt, but he himself was so near collapse that it seemed he was merely flailing at Smetka with his sweat-soaked shirt, not helping. When the loading car came out of the tunnel, he and Smetka were lying side by side. Reffie did not even hear the cheers of the waiting men.

Always afterwards Reffie tortured himself with the question of whether he might have saved Smetka if he had thought of a better way of moving him. But the company doctor said that he, Reffie, could have done nothing—that Smetka's heart had simply stopped. The miners said it was heatstroke: they'd seen it many times.

THROUGH A GLASS, DARKLY

Ah, there she was: Andrés caught the swing of her lilac beach bag as she came into view. Every evening at this time she appeared outside his window: the bikini tied loosely around her hips, she sat down on the hotel retaining wall and bared her magnificent breasts to the sea. It was somehow unnerving, this sight of a gray-haired woman sitting with her near-naked body to the setting sun, it violated everything he had been taught in his village. It was perhaps more disturbing to him because over the years he thought he'd become quite tolerant of these promenading tourists whose families felt it old-fashioned to cover their daughters' nudity from the eyes of strangers: girls so young they'd perhaps not yet dreamed of love strolled the beach, their small breasts poking forth like awkward plums.

Andrés bent again to his bucket, he filled the sponges with water and raised them above his head as far as his long arms could reach. Then he stood watching as the water ran down the glass, blurring his view of the woman. Among his many jobs here—some there were that he'd never liked, and others that were merely dull—this was one he'd come to enjoy: first the flow of water down the plate of glass window, then the wiping down of the glass in long smooth strokes. When he had finished, the glass would be spotlessly clear, he might have tried to walk through it straight to the sea .... He stepped back from the glass a moment, checking his work from another angle while not ceasing to watch the woman. A sparrow had paused at her feet and was now pecking at the coarse sand. The coarseness of the sand at this end of the beach had been a continuing disappointment to Andrés ever since he'd come to work in Torremolinos: he would have preferred a cream-colored beach with many seagulls. He paused, frowning: what was this? She was not leaning back as usual to take in the mellow rays of the fading sun. Instead, tense and anxious, she was fumbling in her beach bag, staring with something like suspicion at the face of a watch—Andrés caught sight of the metal case and the glint of the chain which must lie on her bosom when she was dressed.

.... *dressed*. Andrés could easily imagine how, when she dressed she might first slip into some soft undergarment, then how she might take from her wardrobe a pastel-colored linen suit such as he saw so many women wear while they promenaded on the Carihuela with their white-haired husbands .... This one appeared not to have any such husband to promenade with; but she was in a hurry now, that much was certain. In a few minutes, perhaps, she would pick up her bag and move away from the beach, out of sight .... Andrés too looked at his watch, calculating what he might do: if, instead of taking his dinner in the kitchen, he quickly changed clothes, he might be on the beach before she left.

Never before had he wiped down the great plate glass with such speed, leaving, he saw with a stab of conscience, a long nearly invisible streak at the frame. Then he nearly ran down the stairs to the kitchen—a vast underground community where the guests' every need, real or imagined, was scrupulously cared for. His friend, Ernesto, a cook, showed his surprise when Andrés did not stop for supper: it was considered a perquisite of the job that you could take your evening meal at the hotel. Waving Ernesto's questions aside, Andrés flung off his workclothes and was out of El Oriente within minutes.

Ah, she was still there: but she was slowly, thoughtfully, gathering up her sandals and beach bag. To Andrés' surprise she now pulled from this bag a sundress, whose upper folds she arranged around her bosom; then carefully she tied the halter strings at her back. From a discreet distance Andrés watched and waited. Above all, of course, she was not to know that she was observed, she was not to be frightened .... He remained a good fifty yards behind her as she walked through the sand and up the stairs toward the Carihuela.

It was a perfect summer evening. The sea swelled like blown glass, creating its own transparencies. From moment to moment the twilight-sky darkened: soon the only remaining light would come from the dozens of restaurants facing the sea. The smell of roasting chicken, of barbecuing lamb, of steaming shellfish, rose on the air, reminding Andrés that he had missed his dinner. He looked around: it was not yet the peak hour. There were still many available tables, their tablecloths white as pearls; beside each plate, folded to neat points, like the ears of a cat, poked forth a gleaming white napkin.

But see now: the lady, *his* lady, had apparently arrived too soon. So: in spite of her eagerness to leave the beach, she was now promenading back and forth on the Carihuela, pretending, he thought, to shop (she bought nothing). After three or four turns on the walk, she sat down on a stone bench to rest or wait, facing the sea. She touched the chain around her throat, resisting, perhaps, the temptation to open the watchcase, to check the time again. But Andrés took it all in, saw how she was not able to refrain from glancing down at the wristwatch of a tourist who had meanwhile sat down beside her. *There now! See that?* Andrés alerted himself. *He too is only pretending to look at the sea. Just wait and see, he'll speak to her ....*

And the stranger did speak to her. At the sound of his voice the woman leaped to her feet in alarm or in embarrassment, perhaps, that this stranger should speak to her—that because she was sitting alone on the bench he might think .... At this point Andrés made a supreme effort to enter her mind, but managed only to carry himself to the edge of a brink beyond which he could not follow her thoughts.

But what she did now seemed transparently clear to him: she strode to a nearby phone booth as if, having made some resolve, she must move quickly before losing her nerve .... And it seemed to Andrés moments later when she turned away from the booth that she made her way with somewhat less self-assurance through the crowd beginning their evening stroll on the Carihuela. Even the casual swing of her bag seemed to Andrés a studied artful indifference .... She now walked slowly, very slowly—as slowly as she could without blocking the flow of people along the Carihuela—to the very last restaurant on the walk, La Puesta del Sol: beyond this end of the beach there lay only a dull breakwater with flotsam washed up from the tide. Ah, Andrés saw now that she had paced herself with such deliberate slowness so that she would *not* be the first to arrive at the restaurant: here a handsome young man waited alone. So *he* was the one, apparently, whom she had so anxiously waited ... whom she had so carefully kept waiting. Andrés now took a long look at her companion: at the gray eyes, the robin's egg sport shirt, the fresh sunburn which lay like a soft garment across his throat and arms, above all at the hands holding the glossy menu between his fingers tips, balancing it as if it were parchment or a fragile glass bowl.

But Andrés was now wishing that the two had not arranged to meet here at La Puesta del Sol. Merely to walk past them again and again was impossible: at this end of the beach he, Andrés, would be conspicuous no matter which way he went whether he retraced his steps to the hotel or turned a sharp corner at La Puesta del Sol, bringing him down a narrow street.

He realized that he was still staring at one of those blackboards on which even the more expensive restaurants quaintly offered their *comida del día* (but the acceptable hour for that bargain dinner would now be considered over). Quickly Andrés calculated his options. Suppose he went in and sat down, what might he order? He fingered the pesetas in his pockets: only a few days ago he'd sent seven hundred pesetas to his sister Leticia. Yes, he would go in, he would order a bowl of mussel soup, he would affect a languid air, as if he were suffering from some stomach upset. He would sip his soup slowly, very slowly ... while listening ....

But from the moment Andrés spoke the waiter seemed to take offense at him. No doubt Andrés' native accent gave him away, or even his shoes: he'd heard the desk clerk at the hotel boast that he could always tell a foreigner by his shoes. Involuntarily he moved his feet under the table, smoothed his mustache with what he hoped was a confident air, and ordered his soup.

"La sopa—nada más?" The waiter stared at him as if he were about to say something rude, but to Andrés' relief he merely strode away from the table. He returned at once with the soup. Some of it had sloshed

onto the plate, but the waiter did not lay a clean napkin under the bowl as Andrés was certain they would have done for a guest at El Oriente.

But what matter? He was here. For the first time he was now able to observe the woman face to face. In her youth, apparently, she had been a true *rubia*. Now when she smiled with what seemed to Andrés gross, even pathetic tenderness, the transparent skin became suffused with color. She and her companion sat holding the glossy menus—not looking at them but looking instead at each other. Several times, as if the menus were too heavy a burden, they lowered the menus to their laps. When the waiter had returned a second time for their order (Andrés' soup was cooling rapidly), the young man ordered quickly and confidently for them both. They seemed then to sigh with relief, their look seemed (to Andrés) to say, "At last .... Alone ...."

To increase their illusion of being alone Andrés lowered his gaze, studying the delicate design of the mussel shells. He listened: the couple were speaking English, that much he knew, but with an unusual accent, either British or Australian or even some regional American accent, he was not sure. He strained every nerve to hear, to understand more, as now and then came tantalizing phrases that he understood. "Tell me ...." "Look here, you ...." "I'll be damned ...." "I can't always ...." "You don't have to ....." "Well, what do you want?" Then her companion— quick, acerbic: "What do *you* want?" followed by a deep silence.

An unaccountable joy seized Andrés as he grasped this last sentence. Whatever she wanted, it was not the same as *he* wanted.

Abruptly the silence that had enveloped the three of them was broken. A family party came in laughing and talking. A fiesta of perhaps fourteen people; there was, of course, no reason they should. lower their voices; they had a perfect right to fill the air with their happiness. But Andrés wanted to push them straight into the sea: they were drowning out the voices he wanted to hear. And further, the joy they took in their fiesta made him suddenly aware of himself: neither the noisy carefree intimacy of the family nor the restrained intimacy of the woman with her companion were his, Andrés'. It made him ashamed of being alone, as if he had done something base and his action had been revealed to everyone. He rose abruptly to go. As he passed the woman and her companion he paused, his brain on fire with the need to speak to them, but he barely knew enough English to be understood. Still, he stood rooted beside their table as if he were about to ask for the time, for a match, for a ....

Their conversation halted in mid-sentence. They looked up at Andrés. The woman's hand flew to her throat. Andrés took it all in: the bones of her neckline, the unadorned hand with strong, wide knuckles: no ring. As if absent-minded, her hand strayed to the lilac bag beside her: with a shrug-like thrust of the shoulder she peered into the bag as if searching for something. With this gesture it seemed to Andrés she had dismissed him: he passed their table and moved onto the Carihuela.

Behind him he heard her companion murmur "... interesting ..." followed by a muted, conspiratorial laugh.

For the rest of the week Andrés brooded about it all, asking himself over and over questions that were unanswerable, recalling again and again the muted, conspiratorial laugh. All that week the woman did not appear outside his window; he felt a melancholy loss at her absence, sharpened by the strange clockwork of hotels: overnight there was an invasion of American teenagers who filled every seat in the lobby, calling to one another like a flock of birds. Then the teenagers were followed by a group of Cubans from Florida whose language, after all, was his own, so he could not ignore their conversations: he found himself, rather, listening with shameless attention to their tales of affluence in Little Havana, in Key West, in Tampa .... Their energetic plans for the future made him feel suddenly tired and bored. Perhaps what he needed to lift his spirits was to spend the day with Leticia and his nephews, who adored him—they were always ecstatic to see their Uncle Andrés drive up on his motorcycle.

Early Sunday morning he dressed carefully, wearing his best jacket. With his hair styled in the latest fashion and wearing his new sunglasses, no one would have thought, merely by looking at him, that he was not a guest at El Oriente.

His motorcycle was parked at the rear of the hotel and as he walked toward it he jingled the keys and coins in his pocket for pure joy. It was a beautiful day—a man was lucky to be alive even if he never sailed his own boat in Tampa Bay .... He adjusted his helmet with a gesture that was (almost) a salute to the beautiful morning; then he moved down the ramp onto the two-lane highway. He was just accelerating to what he felt was a perfect speed when he saw the woman with the lilac bag: she was waiting for a bus to downtown Torremolinos. At once he pulled up at the curb beside her.

At the sudden sight of Andrés' foot resting on the curb she took a startled step backward. She turned with apprehension to look back at the hotel entrance.

With what Andrés believed was exquisite politeness, he asked: "Ride, *senora*? Sunday today. Not many buses ...."

She shook her head, not smiling. She had understood him well enough, but he saw that she was afraid. She turned her head away, breathing sharply. Yet Andrés was hopeful that he could assure her by the respectful tone of his voice, by the tender diffidence of his smile, that she would be perfectly safe with him. To communicate this message he went so far as to remove his sunglasses so that she might see what he believed were the candor and honesty of his eyes.

But this was a fatal mistake on his part: her wide gray eyes, the color of seagulls' wings, turned dark with terror. She stepped back, her mouth opened. Andrés saw that in a moment she would scream. Unnerved by her terror, and furious with her for her blind stupidity, he revved his engine and roared away: the fool, what did she think he would do to her? She had only added another humiliation to their evening on the Carihuela.

As he rode like a fury in the direction of downtown Torremolinos, he could see her in his rearview mirror. She was opening her lilac bag, taking something out—a pencil, perhaps, to write down his license number: he would lose his job at El Oriente! In a burst of retaliatory rage at this final affront, Andrés made a U-turn on the highway, passing her on the opposite side. Then with an expert, leaning curve of his motorcycle, he passed her again on the Oriente side. Bending from his seat like some rodeo rider, he gripped the lilac bag. But in spite of his utmost force, it would not yield to him. Instead, the brutal shock of their contact almost pulled him from the motorcycle: the cycle lurched onto the sidewalk before he was able to veer it back to the highway. But to his horror he saw now that the woman's wrist was caught in the drawstrings of the purse, she was being dragged behind him. The sweat poured down his back as with a fierce, heartbreaking wrench he managed to free her, releasing her onto the highway. As he looked back, he could see her sitting against the curb, sobbing.

He roared away like a madman to his room at the other end of town. Still breathing heavily, his hands trembling, he sat down on his bed and opened the lilac bag: there was nothing in it except a handkerchief, a few pesetas, and a business envelope. The envelope, too, was empty. Andrés bowed his head to the lilac bag which held nothing for him, nothing at all, and wept.

MY FUTURE

I used to vow that when I'd reached a man's estate and I'd made a lot of money, she'd quit her job, she'd never again make those wrenching choices between Luxury and Necessity. I'd arrive home bearing gifts that would be pure and unalloyed evidence that we had made it. That was my vow.

For the first two or three years after his death, in spite of her assurance to him that we would make it (*Jeremy and I will make it*, she'd promised him: he was not to worry, he was to be allowed to die without having to worry about *that*) an occasional ripple of fear would cross her face and she would seem to be asking me, asking *me* who barely understood that we would never be seeing him again: *will we make it, Jeremy?* Afterwards,

traces of the isotope ... were slightly above the threshold of detectability

we buried him in Irving, Ohio where he had been born. She returned to her job at the plant. We had plenty to eat, we wore decent clothes, though never fashionable ones, and she had a way of letting me know that she was putting something away for my future. I adjusted to growing up alone, to returning home in the afternoons and finding her, not at home, but at the plant. For several years I persisted childishly in hating the men who would come to take her to a dinner or a movie, for fear she'd marry one of them. But by the time I got old enough to think about girls myself, I realized she had a more exalted purpose in life:

a term that supersedes the roentgen as the unit of dosage. A millirad is a thousandth of a rad.

my future.

Now the fear I see in her face is not occasional, she is no longer concerned with *making it*. She is no longer concerned about the terrible rate of inflation or how strange it seems not to be able to afford things we used to take for granted, like coffee and pure vanilla flavoring. She no longer talks about the food we can't afford but about the things we are afraid

FDA Standards say that 1,000 picocuries are cause for concern and 12,000 would be an emergency

to eat. Yet when I have suggested, as I have several times already, that she not ever return to the plant, that we move away, she only shakes her head and protests with a new quaver in her voice which quite overwhelms her faint English accent, that she has a good job here, that she worked hard to get this job, that good jobs are ter-*r*-ibly (on this word the trill of the *r* restores her to England) hard to find, "We'll just have to wait it out, Jeremy," she says, "that's all. Soon," she adds, "there'll be an *all clear*." This expression is one she has called up from her girlhood during which, when the warning signals sounded, children were led to the subway stations for shelter (some, in the countryside, merely cowered in crude trenches, hiding their heads till the danger

Q. Do our licensing policies take into consideration population density?
A. If a proposed site has over five hundred people per square mile, that triggers a more intensive examination of alternative sites.

was over). The sirens would sound, then at last would come the *all clear*. Safety, like the sunrise, was assured you if you could survive the blitz: you could depend on that much.

one immediate study will be of urine samples of about fifty people living adjacent to

She watches me all the time now, when she thinks I'm not watching her. When I speak to her, there is a sort of heightened comprehension in her face, which used to mean that she was listening intently for a lie. Now it is as if she were awaiting the *all clear*. Under ordinary circumstances this naked, listening gaze would embarrass me because for the past year my voice has been changing. I will *eventually* be a pleasing baritone (that is, if like my girlfriend, Barbara, you think baritones are pleasing). Very soon, our family physician says, my voice will stabilize. Meanwhile

learned only yesterday that another substance, Iodine-131 was among the substances ... Iodine-131 can be especially hazardous ... if it gets into the food chain, because of biological concentration

some residuum, like sand, remains scattered throughout the vocal chords. It's natural, of course. It's not anything I can merely cough away. There it is, my manhood, locked in my throat like a tiger ready to roar.

How interesting it's going to be studying these scattered pieces of oneself—the pituitary, the adrenals, the islet of Langerhans, the chromosomes

said that over the course of ten days there had been 400 millirems of gamma radiation, equal he said "to the accumulated fallout on the East Coast after 25 years of testing."

which carry my child's inheritance. I used to promise Barbara that when I'd become a famous physician I'd come and get her, no matter *where* she was, even if she were already married to somebody else. She liked that, she liked the idea of being married to a famous doctor, somebody who might some day

they are getting 63 curies per second ... which would put us somewhere in the 1200 millirem per hour

be engaged in cancer research. Tried again to call her just now but (of course) her line is busy. Our lines are always busy: the entire high school is on the phone, keeping each other informed, keeping each other calm by talking, endlessly talking. Also, television, radio, even card games, are helping us through these scary yet somehow boring days (would an utter catastrophe be merely boring, after all?) Barbara is terrified, I know that, although her jokes are just as brittle

imbrittled and lost structural integrity in some regions of the core zirconium cladding that surrounds the uranium rods

and grotesque as ever, full of gallows humor. Lately she's begun having her period (somewhat later than usual for her "type" I would think: tall, slim, dark, ectomorphic) and has been cutting her Swimming Class regularly every month. Which must be really tough for somebody like her who all last winter—the worst ever—hiked two miles just to practice her diving in an olympic-sized pool. Whereas *I* would come home and watch Star Trek, then curl up on our living room sofa and fall asleep to the humming furnace till the sound of pots and pans in the kitchen woke me for dinner. Already it seems to me that *that* was my childhood.

critics are aghast at the thought of creating a network of radioactive mausoleums

assured ... no threat of radioactivity in the milk or drinking water

Barbara's line is still busy. Fact is, probably every second person in town is using the phone at this very minute. We don't go out, so our only social life is through this telephone marathon. I think I've phoned every living soul I know within twenty miles of here, *other atomic reactors, including so-called breeder reactors in which the bombardment is so intense it actually creates a greater amount of fissionable isotope than the reactor consumes*

including ratfinks and cretins I wouldn't ordinarily talk to. Anyway, I can tell that this is going to be one hell of an afternoon. I can tell that by the notes-of-command on our kitchen bulletin board. Like a Civil Defense engineer, she has filled the board with precise activities, hunkering down, so to speak, in this, her psychological bomb shelter:

> Defrost fridge.
> Cook beans in press. cooker & prep. for freezer.
> Call Milly, Jo, Stan.
> Check with h.s. principal again (he knows something?)
> Call Hursak: Maybe new information re Evacuation.
> Call Mother (904) 372-1083 Tell her *all clear*.

Since we buried him in Irving, Ohio she has conscientiously reported for work at the plant every day, excepting a few days off for sick leave and for our summer vacations. It seemed that so long as she had this regular work schedule, she was secure—shoring up her certificates of deposit against future anxiety. Deductions from her check were made on a monthly basis: Federal Income Tax deduction, State Income Tax deduction, Group Insurance deduction, Blue Cross and Blue Shield plus Major Medical deductions: all were snatched from immediate gratifications to guarantee her a future without

Four Got Overdoses of Rays But No Harm Is Reported

Our safety rests not on the conceivable accident but on the inconceivable

terror. But today she has twice assured me, the white of her teeth exploding violently in the wide U of her mouth, that there's not going to be any massive evacuation, that there's no need for it. They're keeping us indoors because they're being very cautious, overly cautious, probably. That's the way it is with governments, she says. It's safer for them to tell one hundred thousand people to go home and lock their doors than to take the risk of telling them to do something ... more dramatic. Then, they'd be *responsible*. But her rhetoric seems suddenly to grow slack in her mouth. Words have become a strident counter offensive: they lie to us, we begin to lie to ourselves. If only we could hurl ourselves on this enemy, come to grips with it in the fifth act. Then

and an even greater quantity of plutonium-239 created by the constant neutron bombardment of the unfissionable U-238

108

said ... "There was no capability to review, much less understand the impact of radiation exposure."

suddenly she rallied, made some bitter-comic observation about a class action suit, and went to watch the events on tv.

conceded that he began to realize mass evacuation was a potential

technicians were dissolving hydrogen gasses in the continuing plan to produce a "benign state" in the emissions

What troubles me about all this is that I can longer keep my vow: I can no longer promise her anything. I can't even promise to take care of myself. I can't promise that I'll go on to college, graduate from med school with distinction, and make a lot of money some day which will make up to her for those years of doing without (it's one of her favorite expressions: *Oh well, Jeremy, I guess we've done without it all these years, we can do without*). I can't promise her that I'll phone her regularly after I've moved away from home with my wife and that some day her grandchildren will send her birthday cards, Christmas cards, with pictures of all their kids: which will be a sort of resurrection for her when she will be too blind, perhaps to recognize my

health studies will be long-term ones involving any "clinical changes" or physical problems, and any emotional problems.

thousands of uranium mine workers have died of skin cancer since

handwriting anymore. All I can promise now is that Yes, I'll have a regular physical check-up. Yes, I'll be very cautious, opting always for the minimal number of X-rays for head, teeth, chest and limb. And yes, I may even now consciously have to choose to marry a woman who was born somewhere else, very far from here, someone from the innermost jungles of Brazil, perhaps, who's been basking in the natural radio-activity of sunlight. Someone, in short, who unlike myself was never exposed

items such as pumps, pipes and valves that either have been irradiated or have radioactive debris embedded in them must be disposed of ... cut up into pieces, placed into lead and concrete-lined disposal tanks

and therefore could not possibly have suffered any chromosome damage. Barbara has already said that she'd rather die than give birth to some hydra-headed mutant. Does that mean that we should announce that our (tentative) future engagement is absolutely *off*? This time when I phone I'll ask her flat-out to tell me what she intends to do now: about herself, about motherhood, about us ....

22 dairy farms in the area showed levels ranging from 11 to 46 picocuries per liter ... However ... 12,000 picocuries per liter is the level where regulatory measures

were informed that all incoming raw materials, milk, cocoa bean, soybean and peanuts, everything is

... We never got to that subject. Barbara was full of reassurances. She says her Uncle Hal who is a lab technician and works in Detroit told her that there is nothing to worry about, that They had had a problem like that sometime ago at the Enrico Fermi facility, but They'd handled it all right, and everything had turned out O. K. We talked about the fact that there would be no school again tomorrow. She wanted to know: did I think we'd get in our required number of school days or would we have to go to summer school? Suddenly we have all become passionate and righteous about our need to be educated. Suddenly we've begun to intone our constitutional rights of life, liberty and the pursuit of

the task of extracting from the debris 2 million cubic feet of air and 272,000 gallons of radioactive water

happiness. Suddenly we cynical students have become philosophers and patriots. Suddenly we want to save our nation. Suddenly we want to save our fucking skins.

the Federal Food and Drug Administration sent thousands of bottles of potassium iodide. The chemical is a "blocking agent" against

After talking to Barbara for nearly an hour I drift into the living room where she continues her vigil, watching television in a way I've never seen, pouring in Distraction like alcohol: laughter, comedians, jokes, applause, fill our sheltered living room. But there is the smell of cigarette smoke in the room. Before this incident, she'd given up smoking. I don't, however, scold her for this lack of will power as I usually do. Instead I pat her arm lightly, and settle in a nearby chair. I am suddenly disturbed by the fact that her arm, including the long fingers resting on the sofa, seem to be very bony

scientists said there was serious potential damage to bones and internal organs

and transparent. Also that there are one or two "age spots" on the back of her hand. It occurs to me that she is aging before my eyes, that she will vanish before I will ever be able to keep my vow. Does it comfort me that this incident accelerates

said that those in charge ... overlooked the fact that "radiation accelerates the aging process"

my own decomposition and that we may vanish simultaneously? Not much, it doesn't.

With a sudden gesture of irritation, or maybe of fear because she senses my morbid preoccupation, she suddenly jumps from the sofa and snaps off the television. "Nothing but nonsense," she scolds the darkening set. "I think the best thing is for us to go to sleep. They'll tell us in the morning ...."

set the radius at 10 miles (with a population of another 100,000 people) and finally at 20 miles ... 650,000

I have no desire to sleep, so I merely nod assent without getting up, hoping she won't make an issue of it. I sit staring at the spot where, a moment before, the television image had been visible but which has disappeared like a tiny planet before my eyes. I wonder whether it's too late to call Barbara again, or whether I should just sit here, quietly thinking through a new absorbing question—whether it's better to live hard, drive fast and die young, or to spend the next ten years becoming a Great Physician. Ten years

strontium 90 (half life 25 years) cobalt 60 (half life 15 years) cesium 134 (half life 30 years) as well as ... toxic isotopes of xenon, krypton and rubidium

is a long time.

I, CONSTANZA

Can one be in love with the dead? How can I answer that? I have had love affairs before, I know what they can be: but what sadder than to hear a voice, to realize that you have heard it before, only to be told that the beloved is dead, dead, dead. Even the most hopeless adolescent love had not filled me with such a sense of loss. I said to myself, You fool, they used to lock up people for having these kinds of experiences ....

I had never heard of Victorio Esteban until one cold night in December when I went to see a new foreign film being shown for the first time by an off-campus film group. I arrived early—the film was scheduled for eight—but after waiting around for over an hour I realized that the event was mainly an opportunity for a group of local emigres to get together and talk. As I listened to them I gathered that most were from former republics now run by military juntas: comparisons between the old constitutional governments and the new military were the burning subject of their conversations. Since I had grown up in the Midwest, I had nothing to say on the subject, so I settled down to what seemed certain to be a long wait: presently someone announced that the film would be shown at eleven (no explanations necessary).

Feeling rather exiled myself (my marriage had died that year and I was going through a divorce), I sat brooding over my coffee until, not unexpectedly, the group began to sing together (there is a saying that wherever you hear Spanish, there you will also hear a guitar, and so it was: a guitar player arose with the audience and seated himself at a small, improvised stage).

Being alone is one kind of suffering, but being alone when others are singing is quite another level of misery: I folded my arms with an air of detachment and impassivity, as if I were trying to lock myself in. Then someone (out of compassion, no doubt) handed me a songbook, and although I was not in a singing mood, I made an effort to join in with the others. Some of the lyrics were surprisingly familiar to me: it was as if they had been around for generations and were now comfortable as a blanket one has slept with ever since one was old enough to wake in the night and be afraid of the dark. Still, it was better than feeling shut out from the rest of the world .... So I too sang, or sometimes merely murmured softly.

As I glanced around at the others it struck me that, unlike myself, they had inherited these sad songs through their common history.

113

Apparently, they were keenly aware of this, for most sang with feeling, some with tears. I was beginning to feel more alienated than ever when, suddenly, as their voices rose into a stirring march of a Spanish brigade, something as remarkable as it was frightening happened to me: before my eyes the marching soldiers crumbled; their uniforms appeared to melt from their flesh while they were led to a fiery furnace from which no Shadrach, Meshach and Abednego would ever miraculously emerge. My whole body became tense with fear: it seemed, suddenly, dangerous to breathe ....

Abruptly the guitarist stopped. In the unnatural silence the group became restive. It was as if this absence of song confirmed their worst fears; it was the one thing they could not endure—a silence made intolerable by the knowledge that after the songs had been sung and the film had been shown, each one must return to his permanent exile, his private despair. Someone began to cough nervously, and the intermittent gasps shocked the heavy silence: all waited in a kind of quiet anguish for the singing to resume. And then miraculously the singing did begin again, though not as before. Into the air rose a voice as rich and yielding as a field of grass: at the first notes there blossomed in my head a vision—of a dark head singing, of powerful hands moving along a guitar, of bare feet following a plow ....

We sat absolutely still while the record played to its end. When the song was over, a woman sitting near me crossed herself. She had known Victorio Esteban, she murmured; or rather, to tell the truth, she had seen him only once, but it was as if she had known him. As I listened to her describing Esteban—how he had lived, how he had risen from being a peasant behind a plow to become a great artist, how he had been loved by his people who sang his songs everywhere, sometimes in secret like the Christians in the catacombs—as I listened to this woman, a total stranger, weeping for Esteban, I felt a new sort of jealousy. I envied her persecution, her flight from her country, which had also been Esteban's. I envied her ordeal on the Night of Prisoners when she too had been singing with the others until the news of his death reverberated throughout the compound ....

When she had finished, her companions began to exchange stories—at first cautiously, and then more openly, compelled by the need to share their experiences—experiences which were terrifying to me but to which they listened with a kind of dignified suffering such as one sees among survivors of concentration camps. When finally the film had been shown, the audience rose and drifted one by one into the bitter cold night.

That night I carried one of Esteban's albums home with me, and although it was nearly one in the morning, I played his songs over and over. This went on for several days: had I been twenty years younger, I would have babbled of my love to friends and been heartily laughed to death. But this was no girlish infatuation, it was a spiritual crisis: instead

"Can one be in love with the dead?"

of feeling elated, I had fallen ill. I brooded for several days over the details of Esteban's life. But other peoples' accounts were not enough for me: what I wanted was to breathe the bright pure air of his birthplace, to see the (to me) mystical place of his burial.

Fortunately it was the Christmas season and I did not have to be back in the classroom till January. So, one cold clear morning I bought a ticket to exactly the sort of romantic vacation spot my friends had been recommending for my post-divorce blues. I now prepared to follow their suggestions—only instead of the usual baggage I took notebooks, tape recorder and tapes, a photograph of Esteban and as many of his albums as I could push into my suitcase. I also bought a new camera: when you are going to visit the dead, I said to myself, you have to camouflage yourself so as to look like an ordinary American tourist.

A few days later I boarded a plane with about a dozen other tourists who were astonishingly headed for the same place—a small country which only a few years ago had been bathed in blood and tears and which had now become an excellent vacation spot for tourists looking for sun and endless silent beaches. There, I spent the first day mindlessly visiting their big museum in the center of the city, not far from my hotel, as though trying to disguise to myself my real reason for visiting this country where everyone spoke Esteban's language, their lyrical voices sounding like so many familiar songs played on a distant stereo ....

But on the morning of the second day I boarded a bus to the outskirts of the city where, my guidebook informed me, in the Plaza del Lloros the government had erected a cenotaph to the memory of Victorio Esteban, the body having disappeared. It seemed strange to me that they would do anything to honor the memory of someone like Esteban; but I was willing to accept this inconsistency as a sign of the general madness of governments. At the Plaza del Lloros I discovered that the guidebook was mistaken; there was no cenotaph, only a small square plaque laid in the ground with a few flowers around it. There were several other plaques beside his: of course there would have been others on that Night of Prisoners, but somehow I had selfishly not thought of them till this moment.

The small plaque read simply:

Victorio Esteban (Juan Jesus Ruiz)
1934-1973

It seemed proper to me that his real name had been plain Juan Ruiz rather than the more glamorous Victorio Esteban. That contradiction did not surprise me at all. What did surprise me—although of course it shouldn't have—was that there was absolutely nothing for me to do, nothing to say .... Yet, what had I expected? I recall that it was a very warm day and that I knelt down to caress the tangled grass; also that I wept a little, while feeling ashamed of such indulgence that could change nothing. I took a picture of the plaque with my new camera and turned away from the grave site with a strong feeling of disappointment, as if Esteban had somehow rejected me. For the rest of the day I was lonely and depressed; toward evening I burst into tears and decided it was time to go home. I went to bed early, intending to leave the next day.

But I awoke during the night with a painful constriction in my head—not really a headache, but that sort of intense pressure which comes with extreme concentration. I heard a crashing sound and sat up to find that everything had fallen from my nightstand—notebooks, tapes, record albums.

"Constanza," he said.

Now at last everything had become perfectly reasonable: I was no longer anxious or afraid.

"My name is not Constanza," I said. "It is only a common British name. Emma. My parents were—"

"*Exactamente* ... Emma," he said, in that voice which I can only describe by saying it made me feel as though one moment I had been standing alone, deserted, on some Siberian steppe with the Arctic winds freezing my very bones, and then the next as if I had just been taken some miraculous cordial which made me warm, fearless, ready— whatever the difficulties—to march across the icy tundra. Ah, no wonder, Esteban, they had to silence your voice.

"Perhaps ... Of course *now* you are Emma. But when I knew you ... you were Constanza. In *that* life, of course."

I did not smile. It explained everything. "And you? Were you then ... Victorio ... also?"

He shook his head. "Do names matter, Constanza ... Emma? I came because of your weeping. You would not ... your grief would not ... let me alone." He looked embarrassed; his warm voice was now almost plaintive. "Because of you I cannot rest."

He was speaking what I afterwards realized was a dialect spoken in a very remote section of his country where the peasants still labored barefoot behind the plow, yet I understood every word. Still, that fact did not astonish me more than that he should be speaking at all, speaking to me, of all people.

"Yes. You see how it is. Your love would not let me rest ...."

I was embarrassed; it did not seem right for him to take so much for granted, yet it was true I loved him, it seemed useless to deny it. Had I not come all this way just to see where they had laid him to rest?

"So I want to share with you my history. So that you will know what they, the others, do not ...."

"Ah ... Then there were others." In spite of my feeling for him I felt that the use of this word was unworthy of him, that—if the notion were not too petty to attribute to such a voice—it had been used with the intent to wound me in my self-esteem or to inspire in me some jealousy, competitiveness, with ... my rivals.

"Esteban," I protested, my language for some reason becoming strangely formal, as if I were translating. "It is not necessary. Do not demean yourself in this way. I will do whatever you have come to ask. It is not necessary to arouse in me ... these unworthy emotions." I did not say 'jealousy': it would have been absurd. After all, many women had loved him. Was I to carry on like an injured sweetheart about 'infidelities' of a decade before?

"Ah, no. There is no desire on my part to do such a thing to you. To you above all. I want only to give you ..." he paused, "... assurances. That I sang for you before, once. That we have had this life before. You do remember? ..." His voice trailed to a question.

A tremor went through me. It seemed too I could hear horses' hooves, the sound of shouting, the sighing of spectators, the line-up of an execution squad. I whispered, "No. I do not remember. Please do not force me to remember."

His soft voice softened even further. "Very well. We will not mention that time, Constanza. But Eugenia Van Der Kiepher you do remember well, I take it?"

"No, no," I denied. "I have never heard of her."

Esteban lowered his head and gazed at me sorrowfully. "Why will you deny it? It was you, was it not, you who hid with me all through the years of the war: how thin you were, a bundle of sticks. Yet when I saw you—"

"Please. I beg of you. It was not I. You are dreaming ...."

He murmured: "The dead do not dream. Constanza. They *know*."

I wept. I wanted to embrace him. Though I refused to remember, I was certain now we had hidden till almost the end of the war, in the little sewing room off Eugenia Van Der Kiepher's laundry .... But the rest was too painful. I did not want to remember. For at the end, at the very end, we had all been caught, including Eugenia. Only a few months later the camps were liberated, our oppressors were tried and executed.

I was now sitting on the floor, my tears blurring my vision. Strewn beside me where they had fallen were the notebooks, the tapes, his record albums. The truth was I now wanted him to go. The terror and the memories were too much for me, my only wish was for this conversation to end, for me to be restored to my usual life, to my quite ordinary loneliness.

"And what about Dublin? It was Easter, you do recall that?" he demanded tersely, challengingly, even brutally. "1916 ... And you, *Megan*, ..." he emphasized slightly.

I shook my head in sullen denial. Then it was I who was brutal. Turning my head slightly toward him I said with cold fury: "You fool! You insisted on going. You were *mad* to go ...."

"And the child?"

"Ah, then you don't know everything, then. Not all-wise, all-good, and all-powerful, are you? The child died ...." My heart was breaking, yet here I was taunting him vengefully, when I had come so far just to see him.

He broke into wild sobs, as though somehow he had continued to believe that the child, at least, had survived.

In spite of my rancor, I bled with pity for him then. I had already endured this, I thought, I had no more tears to shed.

"Forgive me, Constanza ...Megan," he murmured.

"Stop it!" I screamed. "I will never, *never* forgive you! ... Then suddenly I changed my tune: "No. I remember nothing," I said spitefully. "I've made it all up just to hurt you. There was no child. No Rebellion, no Troubles. Nothing, nothing, nothing. Except a band of Irish madmen and poets."

At this he suddenly lifted his head from his hands and smiled at me. "... and poets. The same, no doubt."

I too smiled sadly.

Encouraged perhaps by my changed demeanor he now pursued relentlessly: "But Catalonia? You will not deny how we sang and marched and refused to die—"

But by now I was inconsolable. "Refused to die?" I sobbed. "No, you never refused. You rushed toward it singing. Our blood is on your hands, Victorio. You left us, you left us. You abandoned me. Always you abandoned me ...." I bowed my head to the floor.

Then it was that he knelt down and took his albums of songs from my arms (I had not realized till then that I had been cradling them). "Here now," he said softly. "Let us put these away, and I will sing you a new song."

"A new song, Victorio? How can there be a new song? You are dead. Dead, dead, dead," I accused him maliciously, but without triumph, for I was not at all certain that perhaps I too was not dead (without yet knowing it, perhaps) and that mine was a purely pyrrhic malice.

"Yes, I have written it since ... since then ... since the last time. I have written it for you, Constanza."

"Ah, yes. Now I remember," I said bitterly. "You do this for me always before you go away again." (But how did I know this? I wondered.)

He nodded in the wise, patient way so familiar to me. "We are in agreement about everything, I see. Now listen and you will understand everything too, and not just agree with me like a docile, loving woman .... You are free now to understand, are you not?"

"What I do not understand," I echoed with bewilderment, for this part alone was like a dream, although the rest of what he said was as clear as sunlight, "is this question of yours, 'You are free now to understand, are you not?' What does that mean?"

119

"Listen, and all will be clear."

Then in his arms in which there was no guitar, with his dear hands in which the death squad had smashed every bone, so that "never again" would he play his guitar, he began to strum, and from out of the pearled cavern of his chest there came this new song:

Vuela, alma mía, vuela, vuela:
Entra al alma de otro.
Vuela, alma mía, pequeña
    mariposa:
Sé el capullo para mi
    hermano,
Sé la flor, sé la crisálida,
Se la hoja en la cual yo repose,
Sé la larva, sé la mariposa,
Sé la flor en la cual yo muera ...
Vuela alma mía, tú eres más
    que yo.
Tú vivirás con mis hermanos,
Tú cantarás mis canciones,
Tú morirás con mis hermanos,
Tú corregirás sus errores.
Vuela, alma mía.
Vuela, vuela.

Fly away my soul, fly, fly:
Enter the soul of another.
Fly away my soul, little
    butterfly:
Be the cocoon for my brother,
Be the flower, be the chrysalis,
Be the leaf on which I lie,
Be the larvae, be the butterfly,
Be the flower on which I die ...
Fly away my soul, you are more
    than I.
You will live with my brothers,
You will sing my songs,
You will die with my brothers,
You will right their wrongs,
Fly away my soul,
Fly, fly away.

When he had sung this song, he kissed me on the forehead. I rose to my feet, wishing to embrace him once again, words of love rose to my lips in a great torrent. But he had gone. I waited for some sign of his presence until long after the sun had risen, but he did not return.... For months I have waited, whispering to the darkness: Come back, come back, Esteban, and you will sing in the copper mines of Rhodesia, in the velds of South Africa, in the sharp grasses of the Philippines, in the roaring jungles of Uganda, in the archipelagoes of the Western World. But from the darkness there has been no reply. He knows, doubtless, that I would follow him anywhere, but that it is too soon for me to do so, that my round of Karma is not yet done and my task is here. And he must know for certain what I can only hope, that Constanza, Megan, Emma, will again be called to be the lover of Victorio Esteban.

In Memoriam, Victor Jara: brutally tortured and murdered while a prisoner of the Chilean armed forces on September 15, 1973.
Author's Note: I am indebted to the poet, Ricardo Yamal, for his Spanish translation of the song in *I, Constanza.*

LOSSES

All who remember, doubt ....
Roethke

Students from the nearby high school milled around the long counter, haunted the aisles, invaded the booth next to Adelina's, as though they were winged creatures from another planet. They flew from one group to another, their bodies smooth and bursting, their masses of hair damp from the summer heat. Some couples stared into each other's eyes with delight: they were in love, Adelina thought. As she had been at their age. She stirred the ice cream in her soda glass, pondering the question: how did love die?

She always knew when, no need of necromancers for that, but how? That was the question. From the time she had turned fifteen, each Love had stretched its wings in flight a while, then, though looking alive, had stilled its fluttering and come to silence. Perhaps if she had known how to avert such losses she could have done so. But she had not known.

The Wild William, for example. A rhymer, a punster, a prankster, a mad wit foaming over like the creamy sweetness she now slowly sipped. Both of them fifteen: people were not supposed to be in love at that age. Yet theirs had been the First Love poets wrote about, the one that mysteriously blessed all the others. Poking a dissolving strawberry at the bottom of her glass, Adelina tried to recall how that had ended. But she could only remember that by Spring, when William had believed she was pregnant he'd stopped coming to visit her during the night on her family's screened-in porch. Then after the doctor had called to tell them they were just a pair of silly kids and that they should be more careful because next time they wouldn't be so lucky, William had begun walking right by her in the halls of the high school, his face flushing crimson as he passed. Adelina's cousin Gwen, ten years older than she, had assured her that there was nothing personal in it, that it was only because William was too young, that he was merely afraid—of responsibility, debts, of growing up.

So when Adelina fell in love again, it had been with a much older man who wouldn't be afraid. Desmond had been grey and already a bit stooped when she met him. He'd had a hard time in Europe and when he lit one of his strangely scented cigarettes, it was with a watchful air as if someone might resent it. As he smoked he would straighten up, as if this act were somehow brave and meaningful. Then, with the manners of a polished cicerone—nervous, dark, extremely European—he would escort her around the city, showing her the heart of it. Desmond never talked about his past life, as if such a subject required more fluency than he could ever have. He worked for a translation house, translating the instructions of German engineers into instructions for American engineers. Adelina was impressed by this; it seemed to her a kind of magic the way he transformed words before her eyes. Besides, she loved him for being an educated man who had suffered much. Living a marginal existence, always on the edge of bankruptcy, he had seemed to her fearless. Then one afternoon as they had walked together on Fifth Avenue, some people Desmond knew at the publishing house, but whom Adelina had never met, came out of a church. It was clear that they were richer and better dressed than Desmond, and Adelina sensed that he wanted to know them better .... To help him out she'd begun to act more cheerful than she felt (she'd had a miserable cold all that week) and had soon found herself alternating between a cough and a laugh; her voice, strangely strident in the innocent Sunday sunlight, had jarred on her own ears like nickelodeon blasts. Desmond had gripped her elbow, had forgotten to introduce her by her last name. "This is Addie," he'd said simply. Her sense of humiliation had not faded away, they had drifted apart. Desmond had soon afterwards married someone with a great deal of money, and when she last saw him disappearing through a revolving door, she had been convinced that he had seen her and had hurried into the first place he could find in order to escape her.

She had decided then to avoid "intellectuals." So she had fallen in love instead with a merchant marine named Gary who'd just been let out of prison (he'd pushed aside the bartender and scooped up the till one night in an afterhours place, only to fly straight into the arms of a policeman in the joint). Gary'd had a body like a Deere tractor; when he roared over her he made her feel rich, loamy, verdant. Then one day he had shown up at the restaurant where she was working as a cashier and wanted to borrow a dollar from her. Adelina had been angry with him and refused to give it to him. She had only her bus fare with her, she said. Roaring with rage he had banged the counter with his fist and called her a cheap money-loving jew. Tears had streamed down Adelina's cheeks as she begged him to *Be calm, please be calm.* She'd thrust her hand into the bottom of her pocketbook (she could still recall the black suedelike bottom as though it were a chasm she'd fallen into), pushing aside keys, photographs, kleenex, trying to locate the little coin purse in which she kept her carfare. She'd glanced up at Gary and realized at once as he watched her that he himself had taken out the cheap little purse with its few quarters. The mystery of it: why had he shown up that day, staging that performance? Adelina was never to know, she never saw him again.

So she should have been prepared for disillusion when Alman

came along. It was true he was a married man, a fact she hadn't the experience to cope with. Yet it was not the marriage which had struck their love dead, nor the children, nor even the long stretches of misery between the times she saw him and the times she didn't. What then? Adelina stared down into her empty glass, considered having another. What then? She didn't know, but she thought she knew to the exact minute when love had died. It had been after a short vacation she'd taken to Mexico (a luxury he himself had encouraged: and for what reason? she now wondered). She had not let him know her arrival time (again: why?) and he had surprised Adelina by being at the airport to meet her. They'd driven away from the city and by dusk had arrived at an old-fashioned tourist home—one with a wide piazza where one might have imagined misty-eyed honeymooners sitting fifty years ago, lovers holding hands in anticipation of what the night might bring.

For them the night had brought neither pity nor terror, only boredom. Set up for chronic passion they were naively unprepared for what they found instead: woman's condition, a monthly joke too dull and familiar to be laughed at. Toward morning Alman had turned on the night light and opened an exciting-looking paperback with a picture of a nude woman on the cover, a knife plunged in her bare breasts to the jewelled hilt. When it was at last time for breakfast they had sat across from each other (in a diner much like this one, recalled Adelina). Alman had carefully folded his *Wall Street Journal* into vertical sections and checked his winnings: GE, Xerox and Enovid, all were up. He had smiled down at the page.

So she knew when that one had died. After Alman, she decided that the death of love was a mystery, an eschatological force. One could do nothing about it, the loss was irredemptive, pre-elective. She decided to love loosely, caring nothing at all for futures. She floated into several casual affairs like a swimmer who knows there's always another side to the beach.

Then one day she had met Pierre while she sat on Riverside Drive watching the light change from blue to black. He came strolling along, eating pears. He glanced at her. She thought she had seen a certain tenderness in his eyes; flattered, she had decided to trust him. She had taken him back to her apartment, fed him lavishly and let him use her pajamas, which were new. She found him to be despondent: on the verge of suicide, he said. He talked to her for hours, days, nights, about the people who had betrayed him. Adelina consoled him. He would seem for a while to be passionate, then suddenly he would quarrel with her, their embraces were intense emotional trials .... Then one day she saw Pierre on a Broadway corner, talking with animation to a Puerto Rican boy who looked much like himself. No, it was the way they were both leaning against the mailbox, as though to publicly proclaim that they were separated by this piece of metal ....

Once his secret was out (in spite of Adelina's effort to weld him to her flesh by lavish Ovidian rites), Pierre no longer made any effort to disguise his indifference. He merely followed her like a sullen, bored child. For him it was all chores. Then one day in January Adelina came down with the flu, one of those Asian imports with nausea and vomiting. She was unable to work. She lay in bed pale and exhausted, like one bleeding to death. It was then that Pierre had vanished into the city without a note, without an apology. Perhaps he had felt such things were inexplicable.

When after over a month of illness Adelina rose from her bed, she had lost thirty pounds, her flesh lay in empty folds about her neck, her wrists; her hair had fallen out. She wept when she saw the spidery wrinkles covering her eyelids. The neighborhood doctor said maybe it hadn't been flu after all, she looked too bad for flu, maybe some kind of paratyphoid, he said, avoiding her glance.

She needed to go back to work, she was in desperate need of money, but she hadn't the heart to be seen in public. She forced herself to stay home on welfare for a while and found that her solitude was driving her mad: she began taking Nembutals to sleep and bennies to wake up. In a matter of months she had to admit she had a habit to kick and if she didn't kick it, she'd have to pay for it by whatever means. One night she borrowed ten dollars from a man in the next apartment and realized with disgust that he didn't expect it back at all, that he took it as a promise on her part, a contract. That night she took an overdose of Nembutal and woke up in the hospital.

But it had turned out all right. Live and let live: she had got rid of her habit and only now and then went on a binge and bought herself a fifth of whiskey. Only she was terribly lonely and pondered how to solve this problem. Mainly, she decided, it was a matter of her ruined hair which lay in patches, like those of a rag doll whose seams were not sewn on right; and her wrinkled hands: otherwise, the rest in the hospital had actually done her some good, she thought. So she bought herself a bright-red wig which she wore everywhere, and covered her hands with thin nylon gloves. She found that if she did not trouble herself about "love," there was no reason to be lonely, that there were men even lonelier than she who were willing to have an affair, so long as it was easy and cheap. Many were even less well off than she (she'd taken on a part-time cashier's job), and she sometimes was able to think of herself as performing a disinterested service, a good samaritan who gave without receiving .... But as for love, that was dead forever, it had died for the last time with Pierre, she decided. It was not, she announced silently, raising her eyes as if to warn the high school kids once and for all, it was not something which once dead could be continuously revived. You crazy kids, she addressed them with sudden rising anger. You crazy nuts, drowning of love in each other's eyes, what the hell do you know about it? she demanded. There was no answer, she knew, and she folded down the plastic straw into her glass, ready to leave. She would not have another soda after all: she was eating too many sweets, she had a positive craving for sweets.

It was then that she saw the old man as he stood just inside the diner. His cane poised on the floor like a ramrod, he held the electronic door open with an air of authority while he stared around, considering the crowd. For a moment it seemed he would turn and go away again. Then his eye caught Adelina's where she sat in her booth facing the door. He began threading his way through the coveys of kids, his cane held high above their heads, skilled and Chaplinesque.

When he reached Adelina's booth he sat down with what one sensed was proprietorship. "Good. There's room," he announced with satisfaction. He smoothed his mustache with a gentle, preening touch of his fingers.

Adelina stared at him coldly. There was no room, none at all. What did he think he was doing? She'd come here to sip her soda and watch the mooning high-school kids, not to be invaded by this story-book character with a cane and a mustache. All he needed was white gloves, thought Adelina; and she smiled involuntarily.

The old man must have mistaken her smile, for he thrust himself into the conversation, as if he were merely continuing a dispute they'd had together for years:

"Every place is crowded. They need a place for people to sit. Just to sit and talk. In Europe they got places. You go out, right away people are talking to you. Here, they sit all alone and they stare at the four walls. Is your hair real?" he demanded suddenly.

Adelina gasped.

"Your hair. I'm talking about your hair," he repeated, raising his voice as though he thought she might be a little deaf. Then answering himself: "A wig, is it? Nylon?" he added with open curiosity: "Or real hair? They get it from Italy somebody told me."

No one had ever spoken to Adelina in such a tone, not even Pierre who used to question her as if she were a clever gadget and he wanted to see how she worked. Yet from a remembered habit of graciousness, Adelina touched her hand to her hair, forcing a light smile: "Of course, it's real hair. Those nylon ones look so cheap. I hate anything looks cheap, don't you?"

He looked at her long and sourly without answering, so that for a moment Adelina thought he might reply with some incalculable insult. His lips came together once or twice as if he meant to speak; vertical lines cut his lips so sharply that his mouth seemed put together out of bits and pieces. Then she realized that it was not a conflict between truth and courtesy he was enduring, but that he was trying to fix his upper plate firmly against the roof of his mouth before replying. Adelina averted her eyes from the struggle and gathered up her handbag.

"So where are you going?" he demanded with sudden ferocity. "What's your hurry?" And he actually laid his cane across the booth as though, were she to attempt to leave, he would keep her there by force. A flutter of fear rose in her throat.

"I have shopping to do," Adelina murmured weakly.

"Shop? What's to shop? Everything's too high these days. You can't buy a cup of coffee with what they send you. Work all your life and what do they send you? Do you get a check, a pension—some kind of pension, I mean?" he demanded ambiguously.

Numbly, Adelina shook her head; fear of him rose like a fluid to her brain. She began timidly to move around the curve of the cane which was blocking her exit.

"Push it. Push it. What you think it is? A snake, it's going to bite you? I don't like to carry one, but who's to decide these things? One day I fell down in the street. Only from the curb, it was like falling down a cliff. Now I carry it, I use it to cross. I never thought I'd need a cane. Look at me, seventy-eight years old and do I even stoop? But when I looked down, the curb wasn't there, my foot had no place to go. Now I put my cane first, I know how big a step."

Then suddenly his voice softened as though with pity: "You married? Children?"

Adelina was already standing, anxious to leave, but the kids were blocking her way. As if they were doing it on purpose, she thought. She shook her head at the old man, trying to keep her face expressionless, knowing that any sign of emotion from her would spur him to renewed insights, prophecies, revelations ....

"No kids, eh?" He looked at her body as though it were a wine barrel with split staves. He turned away with undisguised disgust. Adelina became suddenly aware of her body rotting like timbers. Then he added as if in consolation: "*Nu*, no kids, no troubles. What good did it do me I had three wives, five kids, eighteen grandchildren? My wives they died: just like that, one, two, three. One tragedy is not enough in a lifetime. I had three. Even my kids, one a *nogoodnik*, I only wish him suffering like I've known from him, and the others all girls. So all the *naches* I got, I wouldn't wish it on a stranger. Eighteen grandchildren and nobody writes me even a line. I get my check, I go to the library twice a week. I *fress* at the delicatessen .... You Jewish?" he demanded, interrupting himself.

Adelina shook her head, wanting desperately to leave, to rid herself of that accounting, accountable voice, calculating his life like an abacus. *Three loves, three lives. Now subtract three, add five, with eighteen as a remainder: what's your answer?*

"Well, you're O.K. anyway," he pronounced. "No hard feelings." He glanced up at her with the eyes of an old dog; his voice died in his chest and Adelina knew, suddenly, that the last thing he wanted was to be alone, falling in the streets, wandering in and out of restaurants, babbling nonsense to strangers.

"You going out?" he demanded suddenly, as if this were a new idea.

126

With difficulty he pried himself loose from the booth. He twisted the curve of the cane till he rested, balanced in its center. Grasping it like a kayak paddle, he headed toward the door. "I'll walk with you a little," he said.

Frowning, Adelina pushed her way through the swarms of kids; it seemed to her a hush had fallen on the diner as they approached the door. At the exit she paused involuntarily, looking behind her for the old man. He came forward, his back straight, his walk slow but certain. On the carpetlike square which seemed to waver before Adelina's anxious gaze her companion paused and tapped his cane. The electronic door opened with a sigh. From between his cracked lips the old man smiled at Adelina, not unkindly, his teeth moving at her like a deathshead:

"See? It's easy," he assured her.

ZHENIA AND THE WICKED ONE

To the poor, death comes suddenly—under the heavy load, or the careless knife, or in a haste to be born: or even at childlike and unaccustomed play. Mama, caught in the midst of the joyous Sabbath, had clutched at her heart, gasped, and fallen away from all she loved. The sirens had roared, the machinery of resurrection had been applied; but cold and staring, Mama had not stirred from her final vision; her eyes refused to shut upon the silent world.

Even to Zhenia it was clear that Mama had been unwilling to go; they dragged her reluctant feet in the dust as they shifted her from the street to the ambulance litter; a small round hole, like a larva on the bitten rose, had already pierced the sole of Mama's shoe; the pale O of mortality glinted at Zhenia's eye as they lifted her.

At once a covey of dark faces ranging from ebony and walnut to honey and pale olive fluttered at the windows of the tenements. Angelina Vittore called: "Jesus, Zhenia, what's happened to your mother?"

Zhenia tried in vain to curl her hand in Mama's, but the cold fingers would not respond. "I don't know. She was standing right here when she fell down."

In falling to the earth, Mama's amber-colored combs had come loose from her hair, and now her long auburn braids lay on the floor of the ambulance. Zhenia saw the driver hold Mama's wrist, then lay the braids, wreathlike, on each side of her body. He scowled as he slammed the door and drove away.

* * * * *

The following evening Papa and Uncle Moishe went to the mortuary to see Mama. When they returned, Uncle Moishe threw himself wrathfully into a chair beside the kitchen table where the burnt-out Sabbath candles now lay in strands of braided wax.

"Ah, that *mamser* of a mortician," he exclaimed.

Papa sank his elbows into the table, staring at the seamed and wrinkled oilcloth as if he had been reading into the future from his own palm. He groaned. "Please, Moishe, the children ... have more respect."

"But *what* a mortician!" Uncle Moishe continued inexorably. "We have to stand there while this so-called mor-tiss-i-an puts his hands on my sister's beautiful hair; he picked it up like this, almost caressing. I thought I would choke him …. But what could I do? You, Yankel, you were crying so hard, I couldn't stop you …. We were all crying, *nu*? You can't stop in the middle of such heartbreak to shut up a fool …. Then he says, this lunatic with eyes like a dead fish, he says, 'Such beautiful hair, Mrs. Kalatov's got, it's a shame to put it in the coffin.' He wanted to *cut* her hair, that ghoul[1] …. Then, just as we were leaving, to make it worse—or do you suppose, Yankel, to do him justice, that imbecile thought he was making it better?" Her father shrugged. "May the cholera take his goyische head—he says to your father that Channa's hair has grown *remarkably* since they brought her in last night. He says it's '*just amazing*,' he's never seen anything like it—like Death was an experiment, and he himself God's scientist …." Uncle Moishe stared at Papa, a filament of fear rising from the depth of his eye. "You know, Yankel, that the hair should grow overnight like that, it chills me …." Then, glancing at the children, and at Papa's reproachful eye, Uncle Moishe spat on the floor three times to show his contempt for the Evil One.

"*Will* you shut your mouth, Moishe, for God's sake," choked Papa. "So the hair grew, *nu*? Will that bring back my Channa? Why do you talk so much for? Go, better, call your sisters, tell them what time tomorrow will be the funeral. For me, it's impossible to talk to them. I can't do more …." With a groan Papa rose from the table, dragging his feet with a strange new lifelessness, as if sorrow had taken root in his bones. From his pocket he drew Mama's star of David and her wedding ring; then he walked like a man in a dream to Zhenia's room where, she knew, he would hide Mama's things in the family cedar chest in which Zhenia had put away the fallen combs—the same chest in which he had hidden away all his life that had any value: his prayer shawls for the synagogue, his passport, his diary of persecution in the pogroms of Russia, and his savings book marked VOID, Detroit First National.

When Papa had laid Mama's treasures with his own, he retired to the living room where he lay, face and body lifeless, in exhausted grief. Everyone, including Zhenia, went to bed, although no one expected rest, but only a sleepless night of mourning.

For a long time Zhenia lay in a silence so intense that she could hear the surf of blood in her ears. Then at last she rose. The rusted springs rasped plaintively as she leaped to the linoleumed floor. She padded to where the cedar chest rested beneath a window, her strained nerves recording Papa's willess breathing as he lay in the living room. A trapped moth whirred by, bruising himself against the screen. Zhenia pushed the screen ajar and watched as his wings whirled away to darkness. Then she kneeled down beside the chest and raised the amber combs to her lips. They smelled of Mama's life, and she whispered aloud: "Mama, where are you?" Then she sat a long while in the darkness, scarcely aware that she was trembling with cold and a new

"Even to Zhenia it was clear Mama had been unwilling to go ...."

kind of fear. As she clasped and unclasped the curved staves of the combs, she considered again the mystery of Mama's hair and the look of fear on Uncle Moishe's face, as though Uncle Moishe believed something unspeakable had happened to Mama, something stranger than Death and having to do with the survival of life in the stricken body. Something both terrible and mysterious: for if Mama's hair had become more beautiful than ever, then how could Mama herself be—? Clearly, if Mama were really dead, then nothing would have grown in the night: Zhenia had seen a dead goldfish once at Angelina's house, and a fallen sparrow in the gutter—on them nothing had stirred, nothing grew—they had been beyond restitution. But Mama's hair had grown.

Last year, Zhenia remembered, before she had learned to read, her sister had read aloud a story about a beautiful princess who, having eaten an apple poisoned by a witch, had fallen into a deep sleep resembling death. Although her sister had assured her that witches do not exist, her best friend, Angelina Vittore, said that they did, that they were part of the Devil's empire and that *He* certainly existed. Angelina went to Mass every Sunday, and the priest, she said, "freed her from Sin," which came from the Devil. Her friend had also explained to her how the Devil still lived in Hell, how He had once been an angel, but now spent all His time tempting people, trying to make them wicked like Himself; that He could invade people's bodies, people's minds—that He could make people look dead if He wanted to .... Zhenia had decided that, after all, Angelina's devil was not much different from the Evil One, Ashmodai the Destroyer, of whom her brother spoke.

The possibility that the Evil One had invaded Mama's body and was imitating Death for his own wretched pleasure brought tears of joy to Zhenia's eyes: far better that Mama should be inhabited by a devil and be alive, than be guiltless and face annihilation.

But what could she do? The time was short; the burial, according to Jewish laws of hygiene, must be held as early as possible, which in this case would be the morning after the Sabbath. Zhenia unhooked the screen again—this time to make certain the lights were still on in Angelina's apartment; then she slipped on a robe, climbed up on the cedar chest and eased herself out the window. There was no use waking Papa: she was not sure that Papa believed in the Evil One.

* * * * *

"But Angelina—just suppose that it *was* Ashmodai, or as your people say, the Wicked One—"

"Mostly we just say, 'Devil,'" interrupted Angelina with an air of injury.

Zhenia dropped her hands, feeling a clumsy despair at her bungling expression: a time of crisis, she instinctively knew, was not one in which

132

to remind friends of their differences. She sat silent, rebuffed. She had not wept when they carried Mama away—perhaps she had not then realized the seriousness of Mama's situation; but she began to cry now in bitter helplessness. If Angelina would not come to her aid, she alone could do nothing. For Angelina, five years older than herself, knew everything. She knew how to write the whole alphabet, both capital and small letters, how to fashion doll clothes out of corn shucks, how to make horse-chestnut necklaces by boring a hole through the nuts with a long, hot needle. What was more, Angelina knew whole prayers from the Bible, not in incomprehensible Hebrew (after a year's effort *Shamai Isroel* was still meaningless to Zhenia) but in Christian, which Zhenia understood easily. Indeed it scared her sometimes that she understood Angelina's prayers so well; it did not seem right for a Jewish girl.

Zhenia's voice rose in hysterical entreaty. "Oh, Angie. Isn't there anything we can *do*? If it *is* Ashmodai—the Devil, I mean? ..."

"Do? You and I against the Devil?" Angelina's eyes widened suddenly with the lust of conquest. "Oh, that would be a good one, that would." And she popped a Uneeda biscuit into her mouth, at once wide awake and hungry. "Of course the first thing I'd have to learn you is a prayer. That's always been your trouble if you don't mind my saying so," Angelina added with a certain air of long-suffering. "You don't know any *real* prayers .... Like this one, for instance, I've been getting it by heart—my father says it's enough to scare the Devil from the gates of Paradise." And suddenly Angelina bowed her head, evoking piety and humility like a mantle as she murmured in a rush of syllables: "Now shall the prince of this world be cast out. PutonthewholearmorofGod-thatyemaybeableto standagainstthedeceits oftheDevil .... Standthere-forehaving yourloinsgirtabout withTruthandhavingon the breastplate ofjusticewherewith yemaybeable toextinguishall thefierydartsofthe-most Wicked One ...."

On the last words Angelina blew her lips trumpetlike and inhaled a great clump of air which set her choking.

Zhenia stared speechless with admiration. "Angelina, you're just a genius to remember all that!"

Angelina nodded as though the suggestion were not beyond probability, then added generously: "I'll teach it to you. Then come next Sunday I'll offer up a prayer for your Mama's soul. And I'll say this prayer against the Devil .... And you must be saying it at the same time at the funeral, right? The power of the two of us will maybe scare Him away. If your Mama's possessed ...."

"Possessed?" Zhenia racked her memory for a clue to the strange word which issued like a hiss from her friend's lips.

"That's when He gets to you. Then he can make you do anything. Look dead, even. Or you might fall down, like in an epileptic fit, kicking, and screaming like a banshee. The only way to ex ... exercise

Him is .... Well, like I say, you got to believe in this prayer with your whole heart and soul." She looked at Zhenia dubiously.

"Oh, I do believe it," vowed Zhenia. "I will believe it ...."

"O.K. then. That's all you gonna need. I seen it work once with a man at the Mission House—he had the d.t.'s."

"The d.t.'s?"

"Devil's tremens," explained Angelina grandly. "Now say after me ... 'Now is the judgment of the world ....'"

Zhenia repeated each phrase after her friend, surrendering herself to an imitation of the conviction she heard in Angelina's voice. When she had finished, she added silently: "Oh Lord of Abraham, Isaac and Jacob, forgive me—it's all for Mama."

*　*　*　*　*

Outside the mortuary as they waited for Papa and her sister Anna to come with the hearse, Zhenia clutched at her brother's hand. She wished she could confide her secret to him, so that at the crucial moment he too could add to the prayers for Mama's soul; but Papa's arrival prevented her speaking.

Papa held open the door of the hearse, urging them quickly to enter. One could see that added to his grief was the shame of having been unable to manage the funeral with the dignity he felt he owed to Mama. The mortician had quarrelled with him, noisily and vulgarly, as he saw it, about Mama's hair. The price of the burial plot had been three times what he could have dreamed possible, and even without a headstone, with nothing but a concrete "bed" around Mama's grave, he said, they had insisted upon several hundred dollars cash, nearly a year's earnings. He would have to borrow from the bank. God knew that he had wanted everything to be done for Mama's honor, without neglect or confusion. He had, just now, been trying to arrange the funeral cars, all rented and black, so that each car would follow according to its occupants' relationship to Mama: Tante Becky, Tante Goldie, Tante Sarah, and Uncle Moishe Goldstein with all their families: then the first and second cousins and, finally, friends. There were to be at least ten cars. Mama was not to be buried alone: absolutely not.

"Only that mortician, a dark year on him, gave me such trouble my head hurts from fighting with him: between him and Moishe I had no peace! He only had it in his head he wanted to cut the hair, to make her look *modern*; he bragged on himself that he's an artist, that *meshugganah*. He said he knows how to fix people up for their grave ...." At these words Papa crumpled up, covered his face and sobbed bitterly. "My poor Channele—I spent more money on you today than in ten years here in America ...."

In a moment, however, Papa pulled himself together, scowling and giving orders with renewed discipline: "*Nu*, get in. Zhenia, you sit by Anna in the back. Don't get mud on your shoes, you'll make your sister's dress dirty. And Anna—what's the matter, I have to tell you?— you couldn't find any other dress?—a pink dress on a black day!" He ignored Anna's protest that she had worn the dress when they left home, he could have said something to her at home about it .... "Mitya, go sit near the *schwartze*, tell him how he should go. The Cemetery of Zion, tell him."

"No need for you to do that," the Negro spoke up promptly. "I know the way all the way. I been there a hunnerd times."

Papa turned from him as if with revulsion at such knowledge. "So—go."

The driver lashed at the engine. Then, perhaps sensitive to the implicit rebuke in the vizorlike hand Papa held across his brow, the driver began a glooming monologue. It was as if, dentist-like, he talked in order to distract them from their pain, but managed only to touch again and again an exposed nerve. Mitya glared murderously at him; Papa's eyes finally glazed into an unseeing vacuum.

"Reckon it'll rain again?" the driver asked after a long silence. "Seem like it rain ever time there's a funeral."

"May the *Moloch-ha-movos* take your black soul!" hissed Mitya in Yiddish, and leaping up, he threw himself into the farthermost seat to get away from the driver.

To Zhenia, who had never in her life heard Mitya curse anyone, her brother's outburst was but further proof that their home had been invaded by the Evil One.

To Zhenia's surprise they emerged from the hearse into the smell of country air. The high grass along the roadside leading into the cemetery gates blew like a field of wheat: the mourners lapsed into a guilty silence at the rise of life in their veins. With a strange awkwardness they followed the pall bearers along the graveled path; the delicate roll of pebbles along the path seemed to startle them; they straggled into the grass near the edges as if to silence their own existence.

Zhenia walked between Mitya and Anna. She had not expected such a shining April day. She had felt, rather, as if there should have been ice, lightning and an eclipse of the moon; but everywhere about her the wet earth exuded a radiance from the morning rain. And now that the sun had come out, leaf and bird stirred; the moist earth dried with a heat that filled one's heart: with grief, mystification—and longing.

In the ten-minute walk from the car, the pall bearers had worked up a sweat, and one could see the relief in their eyes as they eased the coffin into the waiting leather stirrups from which, after the prayers, the coffin would be slipped into the grave. Then they stood up, trying not to stretch their knotted shoulders against the faint April breeze.

Aunt Becky, Aunt Goldie and Aunt Sarah gathered around the coffin as the prayers began. Papa and Mitya stood with the men. Zhenia stood transfixed at her sister's side: Anna was sobbing dry, wrenching sobs that seemed to tear her apart. Zhenia could bring no tears to her eyes, but stood petrified with faith and fear that her work of salvation had come too late; for already the lovely pallid face with eyes like candlelight had been hidden from view, and the box was now being nailed down at the head ....

Anna's sobbing had loosened the pangs of others. Tante Becky began wailing and crying out aloud: "Why has God done this to us?" But there was no answer; not since Job had God deigned to explain His persecutions.

Four men, strangers to Zhenia, appeared at the burial site carrying wide flat shovels. Tante Becky fainted at the sight and Tante Sarah, the eldest, who once long ago when they were children had saved Mama from a fire, threw herself into the open grave.

"It's not right. It's not right!" she screamed. "She was the Baby. I took care of her. I should go first—I'm the oldest .... Come back, Channa, my darling, and I'll go before you .... I'll save you again from the fire."

There were murmurings and groaning among the mourners. They said Tante Sarah was having a breakdown; but after a few minutes of violent sobbing, her Aunt seemed to come to her senses. They lifted the spent and fainting woman from the grave.

Meanwhile Papa buried his face in his prayer book; his tears flowed bitterly on the unseen, unread page: "O God full of mercy, *O el mal rachamim* ... May the soul of Channa Kalatov rest in peace. Amen ...."

Zhenia trembled; she waited for a sign. The time must be right, for she and Angelina must work simultaneously to cast out the Wicked One.

The family suddenly huddled together in fearful density; with a shrieking of leather, the coffin was being lowered into the grave. One of the bearers lurched suddenly, so that the lower end of the coffin stood obliquely in the soft soil; for the last time Mama stood erect in this world.

The sun shrank behind a cloud; the birds fluttered nervously, and briefly the burst of morning rain repeated itself. Small, staccato pelts hammered on the coffin, softened and cunning.

Zhenia bowed her head almost to the ground; with her breath she stirred the dust about her nostrils as she whispered passionately, each word burdening her heart with a hundred more she knew not how to utter: "Now is the judgment of this world: now shall the prince of this world be cast out. (Mama, Mama, I'm saving you ...) Put on the whole armor of God (Of God, Mama, the God of Israel) that ye may be able to stand against the deceits of the Devil (not exactly *their* Devil, that is, but ours) ... girt about with truth (oh yes!) ... taking the shield of faith ... extinguish all the fiery darts of the most Wicked One. (*Adonai elohenu adonai echod*) ....

As her tears began falling now over her clasped hands, she trembled with anticipation, hardly knowing what she dared to expect; her faith rose and fell with every breath. She waited—for a cry, a tearing of the flesh wrenching itself free from some awful power: but there was no sound save the rasp of leather as Mama's coffin slipped from their slackened grasp into the earth. Someone threw the first handful of earth, and the volley of coarse dirt burst like richocheting gunfire in Zhenia's brain.

"Stop!" she cried, sobbing in terror. "Stop! They're killing my Mama—they're taking her away!" She rushed to the edge of the grave, but the exhumed earth which now stood piled high beside the waiting trench, seemed to her now treacherously steep and unassailable, and she felt almost at once, with a self-preserving spasm of betrayal, that it would be an unforgettable horror to stumble down that slope into the open grave; and she sobbed in despair and disappointment—at her failure and at her unsuspected cowardice ....

A strong hand seized her—Mitya's. "Zhenia! What are you doing, Zhenia? Come here!"

"But you don't understand!" Zhenia cried—more to convince herself than Mitya. "It's the Wicked One, the Wicked One who's betrayed us!" She threw herself with all the savagery of impotence upon her brother, flailing at him as if he and he alone were keeping her from saving Mama. And even as she struck at her brother who looked at her with eyes of pity, she heard Rabbi Shutz say:

"*Wass is mitt dem kind?* She is too young. She will be sick. Take her home, *nu*?" And to her amazement, the Rabbi, too, wept, their very own Rabbi Shutz, who wept only for the whole of Jewry on the Day of Atonement.

Her aunts pulled her away from Mitya who had locked her in his arms, as if by the protection of his love, he would crush her into silence. She felt Tante Becky kissing her.

"Are you all right, Zhenia? Speak to us, *mamele*. You see what it is to be an orphan?" she mourned to her sisters, and then suddenly they were all sobbing together at the memory of the pogrom which had orphaned them years ago, so that Zhenia's grief and theirs merged into a single broken cry.

"Too young, too young," Aunt Becky repeated over and over. "This is no place—"

But Zhenia refused to be taken home; instead she tore herself from the comforting arms of her aunts and hurled herself to the ground, giving herself up to a grief which she realized even then was never to be healed, for love could not overcome it: her prayers were powerless and Mama would be buried forever.

Now the gravediggers wielded their spades, and though Zhenia buried her head in the grass so as not to hear the blows, the clods of earth came down upon the coffin; falling relentlessly upon herself, and upon Mama—upon Mama's eyes blinded with the shards of a broken saucer, upon her limbs, broken so that they would lie straight, upon her hands folded in silent longing, and upon her hair buried still-living with the dead, till all that Zhenia saw was the pendulum of inexorable spades and the falling rain.

ABOUT THE AUTHOR:

PETESCH, NATALIE L.M. was born in Detroit where she attended the public schools. After graduation from high school she worked at a number of jobs while attending Wayne State University. She eventually received a B.S. from Boston University, an M.A. from Brandeis University and a Ph.D. from the University of Texas at Austin.

In 1974 her collection of short stories, AFTER THE FIRST DEATH THERE IS NO OTHER was awarded the University of Iowa School of Letters Award for Short Fiction (the judge was William Gass). In 1976 she received a *Kansas Quarterly* Fiction Award, and in 1978 received First Prize in *The Louisville Review* Fiction Competition. Several of her stories have been anthologized and a number of them have been cited for Honorable Mention in Martha Foley collections of BEST AMERICAN SHORT STORIES. Her story "Main Street Morning" was included in BEST AMERICAN SHORT STORIES of 1978 edited by Theodore Solotaroff. In the same year *New Letters* published her two novels, *The Leprosarium* and *The Long Hot Summers of Yasha K.*, as a New Letters Summer Prize Book. In 1979 Swallow/Ohio University Press released a hardback edition of this book under the umbrella title SEASONS SUCH AS THESE. Also in 1979 Motheroot Inc. published a new paperback edition of Ms. Petesch's 1974 novel, THE ODYSSEY OF KATINOU KALOKOVICH.

In 1981 her collection of short fiction about Americans born between the turn-of-the-century and the Great Depression, SOUL CLAP ITS HANDS AND SING, was published by South End Press (Boston). DUNCAN'S COLONY, an apocalyptic novel dealing with the imminent threat of nuclear war, was published by Ohio University Press/Swallow Press in 1982. Since then she has completed another novel which will be published by Ohio University Press/Swallow Press. (That press and Swallow's Tale Press have no affiliations.)

Ms. Petesch has taught English at San Francisco State University, Southwest Texas State University, and the University of Texas at Austin. In 1982 she was a Distinguished Visiting Professor at the University of Idaho.

ABOUT THE ARTIST:

Ross Zirkle is a Minnesota artist who works primarily in linoleum block printing. He has had interdisciplinary projects with poets appear in Minnesota galleries, and is presently concentrating on his freelance work and Zirkle Studios with his wife, Ruth. Mr. Zirkle has illustrated another book for Swallow's Tale Press entitled *The Town of Ballymuck*.